The Great Chicken Debacle

The Great Chicken Debacle

by Phyllis Reynolds Naylor

MARSHALL CAVENDISH • NEW YORK

For Rebecca and Melissa, with love

Copyright © 2001 by Phyllis Reynolds Naylor
All rights reserved.
Marshall Cavendish, 99 White Plains Road, Tarrytown, NY 10591
Library of Congress Cataloging-in-Publication Data
Naylor, Phyllis Reynolds.
The great chicken debacle / Phyllis Reynolds Naylor.
p. cm.
Summary: Hoping to earn a trip to an amusement park, the three
Morgan children agree to take care of a chicken that their father
plans to give their mother as a birthday surprise.
ISBN 0-7614-5148-X
[1. Chickens—Fiction. 2. Brothers and sisters—Fiction.
3. Birthdays—Fiction.] I. Title.
PZ7.N24 Gs 2001   [Fic]—dc21   00-064514

The text of this book is set in 12.5 point Sabon.
Book design by Constance Ftera
Printed in the United States of America
First Marshall Cavendish Paperbacks edition 2003

3   5   6   4

Contents

◯ 1 ◯

The Screaming Cyclone

You had to be four feet tall to ride the Screaming Cyclone, Cornelia heard, but by standing as straight as possible, she was sure she would measure up.

Charles, of course, would only be tall enough to ride the Red Devil, and Mindy simply wanted to ride the merry-go-round, which was supposed to be one of the fanciest merry-go-rounds in the world. But the three Morgan children longed to go to Starlight Park even more than they longed for Christmas. It was all kids talked about at school.

"No! No! No!" their father had told them. "I'd rather be buried in mud up to my armpits! The crowds! The noise! The traffic!"

Mother agreed. "Just *looking* at those rides makes me dizzy," she'd said. "We'll find other things to do this summer."

But ten-year-old Cornelia didn't want to do other things. She wanted the Screaming Cyclone. She wanted to feel her hair blowing back from her face, her lips stretching thin over her teeth, and her sweaty hands grasping the metal bar that held her in.

She adored roller coasters, the faster and higher the better. When they'd lived in Iowa, Uncle Bert used to take them on rides with their cousins. They would try out every ride in the park, from bumper cars to sky chutes, from water slides to twisters. But now that they'd moved to Illinois, there were no relatives around.

"So what are we going to do?" Charles asked her as they walked home the last day of school. Mindy skipped happily along beside them, holding her rolled-up kindergarten diploma to her eye like a spyglass. "Do you suppose Mrs. Delaney would take us?"

Cornelia thought of the neighbor who lived next door and shook her head. "I've already asked. She hates rides as much as Mother and said she didn't want the responsibility."

"What happens to parents, anyway?" Charles grumbled. "Once they grow up, they don't have any fun."

"I guess they're just too busy taking care of us," sighed Mindy. She and Charles looked the most alike, with their round faces and blond hair. It was dark-haired Cornelia, with her little pointed chin and brown eyes, who resembled Father. And right now Cornelia's eyes had that determined look.

"I'm going to talk to Dad again," she said. "Maybe we could make a bargain. Wash his car ten times or something if he'll take us."

"We could vacuum the inside of it too," Charles suggested.

"And shine his shoes," said Cornelia.

"Pull up weeds in the driveway."

"Scrub the porch."

Mindy stopped skipping. "Maybe I don't want to go to Starlight Park after all," she said.

"Yes, you do!" cried Cornelia and Charles together.

"We *all* want to go," said Cornelia, "and we've got to find a way to make it happen."

After dinner that evening, with Charles and Mindy watching from the bushes and Mother reading up in her room, Cornelia went out on the back porch and sat down beside her dad in the swing. It was a warm evening, and Cornelia held her dark ponytail off the nape of her neck and fanned herself with it.

The problem wasn't that Father didn't like to have fun, she decided. Cornelia could remember the time her parents woke her and Charles and Mindy because it was snowing, and they all went sledding at midnight. And the Halloween that her parents went out the back door, put on masks, and rang the front doorbell, asking Mindy for a "trick or treat." They always gave wild and crazy gifts to each other on their birthdays too, and this caused lots of laughter when they'd gathered for celebrations back on Grandpa's farm. The trouble was they just didn't like amusement parks, *in any way, shape, or form,* Father always said.

"How was your last day of fifth grade?" he asked

Cornelia as she pushed her feet against the floor to give the swing a boost.

"It was okay," she told him. "The teacher passed out M&M's and showed us pictures of her grandchildren."

And then, before she could say any more, before she could even mention the Screaming Cyclone, her father began to chuckle. "Your mother's birthday is only a week off," he said, "and I've been thinking about getting her a present that would remind her of the farm."

Cornelia smiled too. "You could always buy her a sheep," she suggested.

Father grinned even wider and propped his feet on the railing. He and Cornelia could look out over the whole yard, way back to the woods at the end of the property where their beech tree hung over the Delaneys' shed next door and a little creek trickled among the rocks. "I bought a house with the largest yard we could afford," he said, "but there's not enough grass for a sheep."

"A horse?" Cornelia asked. "We could feed it oats." She tried to imagine her father riding a horse up to the front steps on Mother's birthday. She could imagine it very well, because last year he had given her a carton of coconuts and Mother gave him a bass drum. The year before that she gave him a barrel of pickles and he gave her a canoe.

"No, not a horse," said Father, laughing. "I'd like to give her a chicken."

"A chicken!" cried Cornelia.

He nodded. "I know a man who's selling his poultry business. It's up for auction, and he said he'd give me a chicken. But there's one little problem: I have to get it tomorrow. Everything has to go. As soon as the auction's over, he's leaving for Maine."

"So?" said Cornelia.

"So how do I hide a chicken from your mother for a whole week?"

Cornelia's heart began to race, and goose bumps traveled up and down her spine. *Screaming Cyclone, here I come!* she told herself. Was this her lucky day or what? She propped one ankle across her knee and looked at her father. "What if I said I could hide it till Mom's birthday?" she asked.

"Ha! You and who else?"

"Charles and Mindy, that's who."

"Fat chance," said her father.

"But what if we could?"

"Then I'd be a heap grateful, that's what."

"Nope!" said Cornelia. "You'd have to do better than that."

"Five bucks?"

"Nope."

"Ten?"

"Nope."

"Hey! What are you holding out for?" asked Father.

"The Screaming Cyclone at Starlight Park," said

Cornelia. "The day after Mother's birthday."

Her father groaned. He tipped his head over the back of the swing and groaned again, even louder. Finally he said, "Well, I want something fun, and I can't think of anything crazier to give her, but chickens have to be fed and watered, you know."

"I know," said Cornelia.

"They're noisy. They cluck."

"I know," said Cornelia.

"They poop," said her father.

Cornelia swallowed. "I know," she said.

"And once I brought that chicken home, I wouldn't want to see it, hear it, or even think about it till the morning of Mother's birthday. If it ran off, I wouldn't even want to know. I wouldn't want you coming to me with this problem and that problem; it would be up to you kids entirely to take care of it for a week. Do you really think you could do that?"

"I really do," said Cornelia, though not at all sure.

"Then you've got yourself a deal," he told her.

And out in the bushes, Charles and Mindy gave each other a high five.

◯2◯

Deeter Delaney's Finest Moment

When Deeter Delaney saw the three Morgans heading toward the woods, he followed, and soon all four children were sitting along the bank of the creek with their feet in the water.

"So what's up?" asked Deeter.

Cornelia's brown eyes sparkled like fireflies. "We've got a chance to go to Starlight Park, but it's going to take a lot of work," she announced. Cornelia was good at announcing. Whenever she had something to say, it came out sounding like the Ten Commandments. "Dad is going to give Mom a chicken for her birthday. All we have to do is feed it and keep it hidden for a week, and he'll take us to Starlight Park."

Deeter scratched his head. "Why is he giving her a *live* one?"

Cornelia shrugged. "They give each other crazy presents," she said.

"And he wants to give her something that will remind her of the farm," said Charles. "She always liked the farm." Charles missed the farm too. He missed riding out to Grandpa and Grandma Wheeler's every weekend for huge Sunday dinners with the rest of Mom's family, where there was corn on the cob, baked ham, blueberry and custard pies . . . No food in all the world, according to Charles, could equal the food on the farm in Iowa. And Charles was always thinking of food.

"So what's the problem?" asked Deeter.

"The problem is, where are we going to hide a chicken? It will have to be fed and watered and cleaned up after. Mom mustn't see so much as a feather or hear a cluck till her birthday. We will have to keep it spectacularly secret." Cornelia had been in the advanced class at school, and *spectacular* was on the advanced spelling list.

They were all quiet for what seemed like a very long time, their foreheads wrinkled in concentration. Finally Deeter said, "Maybe we could hide it in our shed."

"Really?" asked Cornelia, wondering why she hadn't thought of that herself.

"I could ask," said Deeter.

"*Ask!*" Cornelia commanded.

Deeter Delaney, who was as thin as he was tall, got to his feet and leaped over a stump like a deer, which wasn't easy to do in his baggy pants.

There were three things the Morgan children had

discovered about Deeter Delaney since they'd moved here in January: He liked baggy clothes; he liked Cornelia; and he liked to tease. He also liked to play basketball and was usually at the playground in the evenings shooting baskets. But he was hanging around home on this particular evening instead of shooting baskets because his teasing had got him into trouble.

"Some day," his mother always told him, "that teasing is going to get you in hot water."

Well, maybe it wasn't water, but it was hot. That very day, the last day of school, Deeter Delaney had sort of "borrowed" a fourth-grader's pen at recess—a special pen that had eight different colors of ink in it. He'd just wanted to fool around with it a while and see if it could write on the sidewalk when Homer Scoates came back from the drinking fountain and saw Deeter using his pen.

"Give me back my pen," he had yelled, and all Homer's friends crowded around with their chins jutting out. Even though they were a year younger than Deeter, they were all probably ten or fifteen pounds heavier and looked like a wrestling team.

Deeter had intended to give the pen back. He had not meant to steal it. But it was the way Homer sounded, all bossy and mean, that had rubbed him the wrong way.

"Give me fifty cents and I will," Deeter had said, drawing a blue circle on the back of his hand, then a red circle inside that, and a green circle inside the red, and holding it out so Homer could see it.

"You better give me that pen!" Homer had bellowed, his face puffing up like a bullfrog, and all his friends puffed up too.

"Fifty cents," Deeter had said, which wasn't nice and it wasn't fair and he knew he wouldn't get away with it. He'd just wanted to tease Homer a little.

Homer's face had gone from pink to red to purple, and somehow that just made Deeter want to tease all the more. Deeter had climbed to the very top of the monkey bars and held out the pen.

"Get down on your hands and knees and beg," he had told them. "I want to see you crawl."

"No way!" Homer had screamed, and all the boys screamed with him, "GIVE-BACK-THAT-PEN!"

A teacher had been heading their way, so Deeter dropped the pen. And strangely, weirdly, miraculously, it had fallen right down the back—the open gaping neck—of a sixth-grader's oversized shirt, a *large* sixth-grade girl who was passing by.

"Go get it if you want it!" Deeter had chortled.

Homer had huffed and puffed, and all Homer's friends doubled up their fists. The girl had looked puzzled, and felt the back of her shirt, but when she walked away, the pen fell out, Homer picked it up, and as far as Deeter was concerned, that should have been the end of it. Except that Homer and his friends said they were going to get even, and everybody knows that when a bunch of guys say they're going to get even, you'd better lay low for a while. Which is why, in addition to liking Cornelia, Deeter was hanging around her place instead of the playground.

Deeter started toward his house to ask his mom if they could use the shed, but suddenly he turned around and came back. He just stepped over the stump this time, holding onto his baggy pants.

"So what's wrong? Why didn't you ask?" Cornelia wanted to know.

"Mom couldn't keep a secret if it were glued to her chin," Deeter said. "If I told her about the chicken, your mom would know by tomorrow morning."

Cornelia's face fell. "Then what are we going to do?"

This was Deeter Delaney's finest moment: "We'll just hide it in our shed anyway. Mom never comes back here, and I'll help you take care of it."

"Deeter," said Cornelia, "You are stupendously wonderful!" *Stupendous* was another word on the advanced reading list, and Cornelia used it whenever she could.

"And nobody," she continued, looking directly at Mindy, then at Charles, "is going to even hint about any of this to Mom."

"When do you get the chicken?" asked Deeter.

"Tomorrow, and we've got to be ready."

The next day, Saturday, the Morgan children didn't go outside. They didn't ride their bikes, didn't go wading, didn't do much of anything except sit around the house waiting for their father to come back. The plan was that he would take the chicken over to the shed and the four children would meet him there. They were so excited it was hard to sit still.

"For goodness sake, it's vacation!" Mother said, coming downstairs. "Why on earth are you sitting inside?"

"It's too hot out there," said Cornelia, trying to think of an excuse.

"It's only eighty degrees!" Mother told her.

"It's too noisy," said Charles.

"Birds? *Noisy?*" exclaimed Mother.

"There are too many worms," offered Mindy.

"Worms! Am I going to have three children moping about the house for three months just because it's *summer?*" Mother cried in disbelief.

"Well, if we had chickens, they'd eat the worms," said Mindy.

Cornelia jabbed Mindy with an elbow, but Mother was already on her way to the kitchen, shaking her head.

At that very moment they heard their father's car coming down the street.

Charles and Mindy leaped off the couch and tumbled after Cornelia, who was already racing through the kitchen toward the back door.

"I think I feel a breeze," Cornelia called to their mother.

"A *quiet* breeze," said Charles.

"And *alllll* the worms have gone back in their holes," said Mindy. "You'll be surprised, Mom, even if it *does* poop."

Mrs. Morgan stood at the window looking at them as they scurried across the yard and over to the neighbor's. "I have the strangest children in the whole world," she murmured.

◯3◯
No-Name

As soon as they were out of sight, Cornelia turned and grabbed Mindy by the arm.

"You almost gave it away!" she scolded.

"I didn't say it was a chicken!" Mindy protested.

"Listen," Cornelia said, looking from Mindy to Charles, "from now until Mother's birthday you are not to say the name of any animal at all! Do you hear me?"

"*I* didn't say anything!" Charles protested.

"But do you see how easily you could let it slip? Mindy, don't even *hint* at Mother's birthday. Don't even *mention* a surprise."

For a moment it looked as though Mindy were going to cry, and Cornelia realized that if Mother saw a tear-streaked face, she would coax the secret out of Mindy before you could say the word, *chicken*.

"Okay, now," she said quickly, "what is it you're not going to say till Mom's birthday?"

"Chicken," said Mindy.

"Or any other animal," Charles reminded her.

"Or any mention of a birthday surprise," said Cornelia.

Mindy nodded. The three of them started off again

across the Delaneys' yard, through the cluster of walnut trees and the bushes near the back, and over to the old shed in one corner.

Their father was standing just inside looking down at a chicken, and Deeter was spreading a handful of grain across the bare dirt floor.

"A live ch . . .!" Mindy clapped her hands over her mouth.

It was, Cornelia thought, the ugliest chicken she had ever seen. It was supposed to be white, she guessed, but its feathers were dirty looking. Its black eyes, surrounded by pink and gold, were lopsided or cockeyed. Half its tail feathers drooped, and the others stuck straight up in the air like a sail. The red comb on top of its head had crusty patches, and one of its legs was crooked. But then, maybe that was the way chickens were supposed to look. Cornelia had never paid that much attention to them back on the farm.

Then Charles said it: "Boy, is that ever an ugly chicken!"

But Father only laughed. "Isn't it, though? Helen's going to love it!"

Grown-ups certainly had some weird ideas about fun, Cornelia decided.

"It's a leghorn. A pullet," her father went on. "Bet it was the runt of the lot. But she's just about old enough to lay eggs."

Well, that was a different matter entirely. If it laid

eggs, it would be the gift that went on giving!

"I'd better get home or Helen will suspect something," Father said. "But remember, don't come to me with your problems over this chicken. It's your job to take care of it and keep it secret. If you kids can manage to do that, Deeter included, I'll take you all to Starlight Park."

"You won't just drive us there for fifteen minutes and make us come home again, will you?" Cornelia asked suspiciously.

"You'll let me ride the Red Devil? As many times as I want?" asked Charles.

"How about the Mad Hornet? Can we go on that too?" asked Deeter.

"And the merry-go-round?" added Mindy, just to make sure.

Father smiled. "If you guys manage to hide this chicken till next Friday, which I doubt, I will take you to Starlight Park not just for an hour, not just for a morning, but for a whole darn day. You may ride on whatever you like for as long as you like and I won't bring you home till closing time. How's that?"

There were high fives again, all around, but Father wagged his finger. "You have only been taking care of this chicken for about ten minutes," he laughed. "And you have about . . . uh . . . eight-thousand six-hundred and thirty more minutes to go." He gave them a thumbs up and a doubtful grin, then left the shed and closed the door.

Cornelia, Charles, Mindy, and Deeter sat down on the floor in a circle, letting the cockeyed chicken walk around in the middle, scratching at the dirt with her wide yellow feet, pecking now and then at the ground, and thrusting out her neck with each step.

"It's like she's marching," said Deeter, smiling.

"*One* . . . two, *one* . . . two, *one* . . . two, three, four . . . ." counted Charles, and for a few moments, the crooked-legged chicken seemed to be marching in time. They all laughed.

"What are we going to call her?" asked Mindy.

"We could call her 'dumpling,'" said Charles. "As in 'chicken and dumplings.'"

"It's Mom's gift. She can name the chicken herself," Cornelia told them.

But Deeter said, "We have to call her something. Until next Friday, let's just call her 'No-Name.'"

So No-Name it was. The hen made low clucking noises as she marched flat-footed around the floor looking for bugs. When Deeter put his hand in the feed sack and sprinkled more grain on the ground, the chicken eagerly gobbled it up—*peck, peck, peck*—like a mechanical toy, until it was all gone.

"Where will she lay her eggs?" Cornelia asked.

"We could set a skillet on the ground and she could drop her eggs in that," said Charles eagerly.

But Deeter shook his head. "We've got to make a nest for her. Hens like boxes with straw in them.

I don't have any straw, though."

Neither did the Morgans.

"I'll find a box she can use as a nest if you and Deeter will find something to use for straw," Cornelia told Charles.

"What should *I* do?" asked Mindy.

"You stay here and keep her company," said Cornelia. "And make sure the door stays closed."

Mindy was happy to be the chicken-sitter, and while Cornelia went home to search for a box, Charles and Deeter went to the Morgans' garage to look for something they could use for straw.

They thought about using wood shavings or even grass. But suddenly Charles' eye fell on the broom hanging on the wall beside the rake. The broom had bristles, long bristles, that looked like straw, felt like straw, and—for all Charles knew—were straw.

"What do you think?" he asked Deeter.

"I think your mom would be really mad," Deeter told him.

"Not if she knew what it was for," Charles said.

The boys took the broom down and tried to pull out the bristles, but they were fastened tightly. The only thing Charles could think of was to use his father's saw, so they laid the broom over the hood of the car, and Deeter sawed away, bristles falling to the floor like rain.

24

There were footsteps outside, and the boys froze as the garage door opened.

"What's taking so long?" asked Cornelia, stepping inside. Then she saw the remains of the broom on the floor.

"Charles!" she gasped. "Mom's new broom!"

"Straw," Charles said, pointing.

Cornelia had to admit it was probably the best they could do, so they gathered up all the bristles, wrapped them in Deeter's shirt, and started across the yard toward the Delaneys' shed.

"Cornelia? Charles? " Mother called from the back porch. "You're keeping an eye on Mindy, aren't you?"

"We know right where she is," Charles answered.

But they didn't know at all, because when they reached the shed, the door was closed, but Mindy and the cockeyed chicken were gone.

⌒4⌒
Never Say Chicken

"A chicken-napper!" said Deeter, his eyes huge.

"But where's Mindy?" Cornelia wailed. "I'm supposed to be looking after her."

"I guess somebody just walked in and kidnapped them both," said Charles. Cornelia gave a little shriek.

Deeter was already playing detective. He opened the door and crawled outside on his hands and knees, checking the ground for chicken feathers. Cornelia merely groaned when he triumphantly held a white one up in the air.

"What does that prove?" she asked. "No-Name could have dropped it when Dad brought her here. It doesn't mean someone took her."

"Maybe we ought to tell somebody," Charles suggested. "We'd better tell your mom, Deeter."

"If you tell Mom, the secret will be out in five minutes," Deeter said. "Do you remember that big so-called surprise party we had for my grandparents on their anniversary last month? Mom called the newspaper herself and announced it!"

Cornelia began to panic, but Deeter pounced on still

another feather. "Aha!" he said. "Look where I found this one! On the path to the creek, not the path to your yard."

Cornelia and Charles followed along behind Deeter as he crawled through the weeds on his hands and knees like a bloodhound.

"Why don't you try barking while you're at it?" Cornelia said, not nice at all, and was instantly sorry because there, coming along the path from the woods was Mindy, holding the World's Ugliest Chicken in her arms. Deeter was right.

"Mindy!" the three cried.

The little girl stopped, still petting the chicken's head. "What?"

"What are you *doing*? Where are you *going*?" Cornelia demanded.

"I'm just taking No-Name for a walk," said Mindy. "She likes it. She was so sa . . . aaad."

"We told you to stay in the shed!" Cornelia scolded as Deeter carefully took the hen from her so it couldn't escape.

"But she was bored!" Mindy protested. "She just kept looking up at me like this . . . ." Mindy let the corners of her mouth droop and her eyes go cockeyed.

"Chickens don't get sad and they don't get bored; they were born bored," Deeter told her.

Once No-Name was safely back in the shed, Cornelia said firmly, "Mindy, don't you ever, *ever* take the chicken outside again. What if she got loose? What if she ran away? What if Mom saw you?"

Mindy sank down in a corner like a collapsible chair until her neck seemed to have disappeared into the collar of her pink dress. "This chicken isn't any fun," she complained.

"It's not *supposed* to be fun for us, it's supposed to be fun for Mother. All we have to do is take care of it till next Friday," Cornelia told her. "What will be *fun* is going to Starlight Park! What will be *fun* is riding the Screaming Cyclone!"

"There's a new haunted house at the park, I heard, with mummies popping up out of coffins," said Deeter.

"I heard there was a Whirl-o-Wheel, where the bottom drops out and you're held against the wall by central force," said Charles.

"*Centrifugal* force," Cornelia told him.

"Well, *I* just want the merry-go-round," said Mindy. "I want to ride the biggest, bestest horse there is with silver tassels on his head."

"You shall have rings on your fingers and bells on your toes as well," Cornelia promised, "*if* we can keep this chicken a secret." She took the sturdy square box she had brought and set it on its side in one corner of the shed. Then Charles and Deeter put the broom bristles in it to make a nest.

"There!" Charles said to the hen. "Go lay an egg. What are you waiting for?"

"A *golden* egg," said Deeter, grinning.

The cockeyed chicken waddled crazily around some more but paid no attention to the nest.

"Mom's going to love her," said Cornelia. "Knowing Mom, she'll probably buy her a collar and leash and take her for walks! I wish this could be our present for her too."

"What *are* we giving Mom for her birthday?" Charles asked.

"I don't have any ideas yet," Cornelia said, and turned to Mindy. The little girl shrugged and shook her head.

Deeter studied them for a moment. "Well, *anyone* can give a chicken," he said, "but what about giving her a *trained* chicken? A *performer* chicken? If your mom likes zany gifts, that would be perfect. Then you could claim it's your present too."

"Trained to do what?" asked Cornelia. "We've only got a week."

"I'll think of something," said Deeter.

They watched the chicken some more. "Well," said Charles after a while. "She's been fed and she's got a nest. What else do chickens need?"

"Water," said Cornelia.

"Then let's get some," said Charles. But they dared not leave No-Name alone with the sack of feed Father had bought for her, so Deeter got a large square cooler from his house, put it on the floor of the shed, and they stored the feed in there. When they left the shed, they were careful to close the door behind them, but they had not gone halfway up the Delaneys' backyard when they came face-to-face with Deeter's mom.

"What are you kids doing back here?" she asked.

Cornelia, Charles, and Mindy stood like rocks, their mouths shut tight.

Deeter answered for them. "Playing," he said.

"Playing what? You're usually out front riding your bikes or something. What kind of game?" his mother asked.

"Chicken," said Deeter.

The rocks were speechless, and Mindy gave a little gasp at the sound of the forbidden word.

But Mrs. Delaney said, "Chicken? We used to play that game when I was growing up. We'd all try something scary and see who dropped out first. You kids aren't doing anything dangerous, are you?"

"No," said Cornelia. "Really. We're just having fun."

"I don't want any broken arms or legs this summer," Mrs. Delaney said. "Here, Deeter. Help me pick some beans." She handed him a bucket, and he gave a quick thumbs up to the Morgans as he followed her around to the garden at the side of the house.

Cornelia, Charles, and Mindy headed for their own yard. "Whew! That was close!" said Charles.

"*Too* close!" said Cornelia. "Now remember, Mindy.

Don't say the word 'chicken.' Don't say the name of any animal at all."

"I *won't!*" Mindy said, frowning. "I told you I wouldn't!"

Mother called them to dinner about six. "We're having Chinese take-out food," she said. "I thought we'd celebrate the start of summer vacation."

"Yea!" said Charles, who would rather eat than do almost anything else, and quickly began opening the little white boxes with the wonderful smells.

"What would you like, Mindy? The cashew chicken or lamb with spring onions?" asked Mother.

Mindy started to answer, then pressed her lips together tightly.

Mother asked again. "Which do you want? Chicken or lamb?"

There was silence at the table. Everyone stared at Mindy. Cornelia knew exactly what was the matter.

"Point, Mindy," Cornelia said.

Mindy pointed to the lamb.

"She wants lamb," said Charles.

"What are you, the interpreter?" asked Dad.

"Just eat," said Charles. "Pass the rice, please."

○5○

Ghost Feathers

All the months Charles had been waiting for summer vacation, he had thought he would stay up until midnight as soon as school was out. He would make popcorn every evening, he'd told himself, eat ice cream, and watch his favorite shows on TV. He would read all the books he hadn't had time to read before—*Who Kidnapped the Sheriff?* and *The Grand Escape*, and he would sleep till noon, if he wanted.

That was B.C., however—Before Chicken. Just one day of worrying about that stupid bird, and Charles felt incredibly tired. He made popcorn and ate ice cream, but when it came time to watch TV, he fell asleep, and at last he dragged himself off to bed.

He fell asleep so early, in fact, that sometime in the night he woke feeling not very tired at all. Or perhaps it was a thunking noise that woke him—a soft, little thud that started and stopped, started and stopped.

The chicken? The only way a chicken could make that much noise was to put on clogs and dance, Charles decided.

The door! Maybe he hadn't shut the shed door after

he'd given the chicken some water. *Had* he shut the door? Charles couldn't remember. Maybe it was banging in the breeze.

He got out of bed in his pajamas with the racing cars on them, pulled on his sneakers, and went downstairs. He took Dad's flashlight from the shelf in the kitchen. Outside, the beam made a round yellow sphere on the ground ahead of him, and he followed it as far as the lilac bush, then cut over into Deeter's backyard, around the cluster of walnut trees, and down the path to the shed.

Suddenly he stopped for, just as he had feared, the shed door was open eight inches or so, swinging in the breeze. When Charles shone the light inside, No-Name was gone.

Charles stood there in his untied sneakers, softly banging his head against the door frame in despair. He tried to think of the worst thing that could possibly happen: Cornelia would never speak to him again, Deeter would call him a jerk, and Mindy would cry, that's what. He could kiss Starlight Park good-bye.

He walked around the shed and checked the creek and the path to the woods, shining the light all around him. Here and there he found a white feather, a ghost feather, it seemed, of a cockeyed chicken that had disappeared. A runt of a chicken without a name. But no chicken.

Second thought: Deeter was playing a trick on him.

Deeter was full of tricks. If he wasn't teasing some-one at school, he was teasing Cornelia or Mindy, so maybe it was Charles's turn now to be teased.

Feeling somewhat better, he went back home, decid-ing he'd wait till morning to start worrying. The air was filled with familiar night noises—the chirp of crickets, the rustle of wind in the beech tree, the yip of a dog in the distance, and the sound of Mr. Hoover's car turning up the street.

The Hoovers lived on the other side of the Mor-gans', and Mr. Hoover worked the night shift at the newspaper. When they first moved here, Mom had said she could set her watch, almost, by the sound of Mr. Hoover coming home from work at twelve-thirty in the morning.

Just as Charles reached the back porch, however, there was a sudden squeal of brakes, and then a loud exclamation from Mr. Hoover:

"Jumping Juniper!"

Charles crept around the house and stared at Mr. Hoover's big green Buick which had stopped at an odd angle in the driveway next door, the headlights still shining on the garage.

The door to the Hoovers' house opened, and out came Mrs. Hoover in a purple robe with big blue flowers on it.

"Harry?" she called. "What's the matter?"

"I just saw a chicken!" came the man's voice from the car.

His wife came down the steps and over to the driveway. "You *what?*"

"A chicken! A chicken walked right in front of my car. I almost hit it."

Mrs. Hoover bent down and stared through the open window of the Buick. "Harry Hoover, I think you're much too tired. You'd better get yourself to bed."

"Ethel, I tell you I saw a chicken! It was strutting right across our driveway like it owned the place. I almost ran into it." And then he added, "It was the ugliest chicken I ever saw in my life."

Mrs. Hoover crossed the driveway in front of the car. Charles watched her bend down and look under the car. She even went around behind and checked the tailpipe.

"Well, there's no chicken here now. You'd better get inside and go to bed," she told him.

The car lights went off at last, the Hoovers went inside, and as soon as the door closed behind them, Charles ran quickly around their house to the other side to look for No-Name. She was nowhere to be found. They should have called her Nowhere.

How could this *happen?* Charles wondered. Chickens weren't roadrunners, after all. They poked about a barnyard clucking and pecking, but they didn't just disappear. They didn't fly very high or very far, they didn't swim, and it was generally not too hard for Grandma Wheeler, back in Iowa, to catch one for Sunday dinner if she put her mind to it.

After searching for half an hour, Charles gave up and walked home. He went to his room and lay down on the bed, wondering what he would say to Cornelia. It was what Cornelia would say to him, however, that was upsetting: *Charles Morgan, I will never speak to you for the rest of my entire life*, was what she would probably say.

That's exactly what she said the next morning when Charles told her. He imagined himself going off to war as a soldier and Cornelia wouldn't even wave. He imagined her marrying Deeter some day, and even at the wedding, she wouldn't tell him good-bye.

"Can we go feed No-Name now?" he heard Mindy whisper softly to Cornelia.

And just as softly he heard Cornelia answer, "No, Mindy, because our stupid no-brain of a brother left the door of the shed open last night, and No-Name got out, but we're *still* not saying a word about it to Mother in case we find the chicken before her birthday."

And just as expected, Mindy started to cry but stopped when they saw Mother coming back from the garage holding her new broom without any bristles.

"What happened to *this?*" she demanded.

Charles closed his eyes. Let them take him out and shoot him. What did it matter? "I did it," he said.

"*Why?* Why on earth would a supposedly normal boy take his mother's best broom and cut off all the bristles?" she asked.

"I sawed them off," Charles confessed. "It was just an experiment."

"An experiment to drive me out of my mind?" said Mother.

"No, I'll buy you a new one, I promise. I'll work to pay it off," Charles told her.

Mother looked at him strangely. "All right. Since you like to saw so much, you can start on that pile of brush and branches at the back of the yard. Saw them into four-foot lengths and put them in the trash. Honestly, Charles! It's not your fault you were born to nutty parents, but I never did anything *this* crazy!"

Charles set to work at the back of the yard, and when he was through, he plodded reluctantly over to the shed next door. Might as well let Deeter yell at him too, and get it over with.

"I really thought I'd locked the door," he told the others as the four children stood inside the shed planning a search mission. "I can't imagine myself dumb enough not to do it."

"*I* can," said Cornelia.

Deeter didn't say anything at all, perhaps because he

knew of someone who was dumb enough to borrow a multicolored pen and drop it down the back of a sixth-grade girl.

Cornelia gravely handed both boys a pillowcase and kept one for herself. "We're each going to search a different place," she said. "Mindy, you stay here and watch in case No-Name comes back. If she does, take a handful of feed from the sack, and make a trail right back to the shed for her to follow. When she gets inside, *close the door!* Charles, you take the path along the creek as far as the highway, I'll take the path the other way, and Deeter, you look in the woods."

When Cornelia wanted to sound bossy, Charles thought, she could do it better than anyone. She could sound like a president and a general both at the same time. He set out, the pillowcase under his arm, and was sure he would never forget this mistake the rest of his life. When he graduated from high school, someone would undoubtedly write in his yearbook, *To Charles: may all your chickens come home to roost.*

Charles himself had no idea what that meant, but Grandma Wheeler used to say it whenever her grandchildren did something they shouldn't. Sometimes she even said it when *Mother* did something crazy, like the time she taught Grandpa's big golden retriever to jump into her lap when she sat down. "Sometime you're not going to want him to do that, Helen,"

Grandma had said. "Watch out, or all your chickens may come home to roost."

Isn't that what chickens were supposed to do? Charles had asked his dad about it, and Dad said that Grandma meant you may do something you'll be sorry for later. But that advice didn't seem to trouble Dad at all, for the very next day he got the wild idea to buy a huge bunch of bananas wholesale. Charles had never seen so many bananas all in one bunch, the way they grew on trees. The bananas began to ripen all at once, however, and the whole family worked at making a huge batch of banana pudding. Then they invited the neighbors in and had a party. Everyone thought it a wonderful idea. How come none of the mistakes Charles made seemed to turn out right?

Now, as he headed up the path with the pillowcase, he made little clucking noises in his throat, hoping to lure No-Name out of wherever she was hiding. Was this the way he wanted to spend his vacation? Was this what he was born to do? When he saw the highway in the distance and the arch beneath where the creek flowed through to the other side, he was almost afraid to walk up the bank for fear he would see a dead chicken on the pavement above, a flat chicken, a round flat pancake of feathers and feet.

He put one hand over his face when he reached the top, shut his eyes as a truck rolled past, then slowly peered through his fingers.

There was something on the road, all right—a flat pancake of feet and fur. But it was black and white and smelly, and Charles didn't know whether to be glad or sorry. If it could happen to a skunk, it could happen to a chicken. He held his breath until he was down the bank again, and then walked slowly back to the shed.

○6○
A Very Close Call

Neither Cornelia, Deeter, nor Mindy had seen the chicken either. The four trudged back to the Morgans' to find Father standing on the porch. Cornelia started to tell him what had happened and then remembered their agreement: *If the chicken was missing, he didn't want to know about it.* Not until just before Mom's birthday, anyway. It was their job to keep it secret and safe.

Father was carrying a suitcase in one hand and his sample case in the other and wore a big grin on his face. He worked for an advertising company, and his favorite line, when he walked into a business, was "How are you going to say 'Merry Christmas' to your favorite customers this year?" Then he would suggest a paperweight with a company's name on the front in silver, or a calendar with a company's name in gold. He would open his sample case to show the latest line of ballpoint pens and calendars and letter openers.

But right now he was saying, "I'm off to Peoria and Kankakee, but I'll be back on Thursday." He winked and tapped Cornelia on the head with his sample case.

"Keep that chicken under your hat!" he said.

She gave him a faint smile and watched him back his car out of the driveway and head off down the street with a little toot of the horn. The four children sat down glumly on the front steps, heads in their hands.

"Good-bye, Starlight Park," said Deeter. "Good-bye, Mad Hornet."

"Good-bye, Red Devil and Whirl-o-Wheel and cotton candy and hot dogs," said Charles.

"Good-bye, horse with the tassels on its head!" said Mindy, in a sorrowful voice. "I'll never get to ride you after all."

"Oh, stop it, all of you!" said Cornelia. "No-Name might come back yet. What we have to do is leave the shed door open in case she goes in looking for food."

Not with all those bugs and worms she's got to eat in the woods, thought Charles.

Deeter's mom came walking across the front lawn. "Helen! Helen!" she called.

Mother came to the front door to see what she wanted.

Mrs. Delaney stood there in her shorts and sandals with a big smile on her face. She was as tall and skinny as the new tree by the side of the house.

"Helen, I know that your Tom is off on a business trip, so I want you and the children to come over and have dinner with Deeter and me tonight."

"That sounds wonderful, Marjorie!" said Mother. "We'd love to."

"The most marvelous dinner just dropped right into my lap, practically," Mrs. Delaney went on. "We're going to have fried chicken."

"Chicken?" gulped Charles.

"No!" cried Cornelia, leaping to her feet, while Mindy suddenly broke into tears.

Mrs. Morgan stared at her daughters. "What in the world . . . ? Have you girls gone mad?"

But even Deeter was upset. "You didn't have to kill it, Mom!" he said.

Now Mrs. Delaney was staring. "Good grief, *somebody* killed it, but it wasn't me. I went to the supermart this morning, and the price of fryer chickens was so low I just had to get some. Bought two, in fact. Is your family vegetarian, Helen?"

"Not that I know of," said Mother, "but around our house, anything could happen." She turned to her daughters again. "What got *into* you?"

Cornelia looked chagrined. "I don't know, Mother. We're discombobulated today, I guess. Sorry, Mrs. Delaney."

Charles was glad to know that somebody else could do something as stupid as leaving a shed door open, and could hardly keep from laughing.

But Cornelia was beside herself. When the mothers

had gone inside to visit, she said, "We almost gave it away, Deeter! If we can't keep it secret, how can Mindy?"

"I don't know," he said. "Like your mom says, almost anything could happen. Between now and Friday, in particular. Especially if you're discombobulated. Whatever *that* means."

Mindy started to get up and go in the house for an ice cream bar, but found she had to pull to get away from the step.

"Yuck!" she cried, discovering that she had sat on a big wad of freshly chewed gum.

"*Deeter!*" Cornelia scolded, when she saw a smile spread slowly across her friend's face.

"Sorry," said Deeter, but he wasn't. Not very. A guy who couldn't shoot baskets till the trouble with Homer Scoates blew over had to have something to do.

At dinner that evening, the Morgan children arrived in fresh shirts with clean faces. Mrs. Delaney had prepared the best dinner that Charles had eaten in some time: fried chicken, mashed potatoes with gravy, green beans, pickles, and for dessert, a blueberry cobbler with thick cream.

Deeter's mom towered over her end of the table.

"How are you liking it here now, Helen?" Mrs. Delaney asked. "Feeling settled?"

"Well, I *do* miss Dad's farm, but Tom enjoys his new

job so much that it was worth the move."

"What you need is to get active in the Women's Garden Club," Mrs. Delaney said. "We'd be glad to have you. And of course there's the choir at church and the book discussion group."

"Oh, I've got plenty to do just getting the house fixed up," said Mother. "There's never a dull moment with these kids to look after." She and Deeter's mother talked on about the price of milk and the best way to grow tomatoes, while the Morgan children enjoyed their dinner and Charles took seconds on everything.

Cornelia had just taken a bite of the warm blueberry cobbler when she thought she heard a noise outside the window—a noise like a gentle *scratch, scratch, scratch*. She took another bite and listened.

Scratch, scratch, scratch. The noise came again. This time Charles heard. He looked at Cornelia.

And then they both heard a low *cluck, cluck, cluck.*

The mothers were talking about peach preserves, and Cornelia rose quietly from her chair.

"Excuse me," she said, "but I have to go to the bathroom." She started toward the front door.

"It's right at the top of the stairs to your left, dear," said Mrs. Delaney, but Cornelia was outside in an instant.

Deeter's mom turned to Mother. "She doesn't like our bathroom?"

Mother looked embarrassed. "She just feels more comfortable in our own, I guess," she said.

Charles got up next. "I have to go to the bathroom, too," he said.

"What is it? My cobbler?" Mrs. Delaney asked in alarm.

Then Deeter stood up. "Excuse me," he said.

"Deeter Delaney, if you want the bathroom, you use it over here," ordered his mother, but Deeter went outside too, and finally only Mindy was left. She didn't know what her sister and brother were up to, but right now she didn't care. She was blueberry from the tip of her nose to the end of her chin, and there was a circle of ice cream around her mouth. She had never tasted anything so delicious.

Cornelia was the first to reach the side of the house, and she could hear the grown-ups talking through the open window. There, right by the flower bed, was No-Name as though nothing had happened. Cornelia put her finger to her lips as Deeter and Charles came up behind her.

"Shhhh," she whispered. "They can't see her from here. Get some feed from the shed and let's try to lure her back there. If we grab her, she might squawk."

Charles knew that this was a chance to redeem himself. He ran to the shed, filled his pockets with feed, and was back in a flash.

They made a thin trail of feed from where the

crooked-legged chicken was standing and on around the house. Slowly, slowly the chicken pecked her way along the ground until finally—*finally*—she was out of range of the dining room window and Deeter pounced. A minute later she was in the shed once again with the door latched behind her.

Cornelia let her shoulders go limp and collapsed on the ground outside the shed. She and Charles and Deeter smiled at each other in relief.

"Did No-Name come back?" came Mindy's voice as she ambled through the walnut trees, her face still streaked with blueberry.

"Yes, and you mustn't say a word about it to anyone!" Cornelia warned her.

Mindy clapped her hands delightedly, and they started toward the house again to finish their dessert. But when they came around the bushes, they saw Mrs. Delaney and Mother standing on the back steps.

"What are you kids up to?" asked Mother. "You're always out there by the creek."

"We're sort of making a summer camp. A place to hang out when it's hot," Deeter said.

"Actually," added Cornelia, "we were just waiting for you and Mrs. Delaney to finish your dinner, and then we were coming in to do the dishes for you. After a dinner like that, the cook deserves a little rest."

"Well, now isn't that nice?" said Deeter's mom. "I think we'll just take them up on that, Helen."

Cornelia's mother shook her head. "I will never understand my children if I live to be one hundred. They can be totally mad one minute and charming the next."

"Well, let's go back in the living room and put our feet up," said Mrs. Delaney.

They did, leaving Cornelia, Charles, Deeter, and Mindy staring at the pots and pans in the kitchen.

"You and your big mouth," muttered Charles.

But Cornelia only grinned happily. "Think *Red Devil*. Think *Screaming Cyclone*. Think cotton candy and Ferris wheel and bumper cars and haunted house."

It *did* make a difference to put their minds on something else, they discovered as they worked.

"I heard the Red Devil goes a hundred miles an hour," said Charles.

"I heard there's a real petrified hand in the haunted house," said Deeter.

"I heard that there's a straight vertical drop on the Screaming Cyclone," said Cornelia, handing a soapy pan to Charles. "I think when we get to Starlight Park, I'll buy an all-day ticket to the Cyclone and not ever get off till closing time."

○7○

Camping Out

After the Morgans went back home, with Deeter tagging along in his baggy pants, the four children sprawled on the grass in the dusk.

"I wish Mom's birthday was tomorrow," said Charles. "No-Name's going to drive us nuts."

"Just five more days," said Cornelia. "We're doing fine."

Mother called Mindy to come in for her bath, but the others chased after fireflies for a while. Cornelia liked to put them on her hands like jewelry, and see them sparkle before they flew away. Deeter caught a firefly and put it in Charles's ear. The firefly crawled down inside, and Cornelia had to hold a flashlight by his ear for five minutes to lure the bug out.

"*Deeter!*" she complained. "One of these days your teasing is going to get us in trouble!"

"Sorry," said Deeter, but what was a little bug, after all?

On the other side of the Morgans', Mr. and Mrs. Hoover came out on their patio to enjoy the evening breeze.

"You'll never guess what we saw cross our yard about dinnertime," Mr. Hoover called over to Cornelia, Charles, and Deeter.

"What?" asked Charles.

"A fox," Mr. Hoover said.

"A fox? Here?" gasped Cornelia.

"Yep. A little red fox. Ran right across the yard and toward the trees in back. It's after something, I can tell you."

Mrs. Hoover laughed. "First he says he saw a chicken, and now he says he saw a fox. If you ask me, my husband needs a new pair of glasses. Only thing *I've* seen is a bunch of boys hanging around back there in the woods, one of them with a pair of binoculars. Playing spy, I'll bet."

Deeter gulped. He had no doubt that the boys Mrs. Hoover had seen were Homer Scoates and his gang, and they weren't *playing* spy, they were *spying!* What he said to Cornelia, however, was, "Hoo boy! That fox is after something, all right, and we know what it is."

"It can't get in the toolshed, though, can it?" whispered Charles.

"There's no floor in the shed, that's what's worrying me," Deeter told him. "All that fox has to do is dig a hole in the dirt on the outside and crawl under. Then he's got breakfast, lunch, and dinner just waiting for him."

"What are we going to *do?*" cried Cornelia.

"Well, *I* sure can't bring it in *my* house," said

Deeter. "The only thing I can think of is to take turns sleeping in the shed with it. Tell our moms we're camping out. I'll go first."

"Oh, Deeter, *would* you?" asked Cornelia gratefully.

"Sure," he said. "Whatever you want."

Mrs. Delaney called Deeter to come home, and when he told her he wanted to camp out, she said that was fine as long as he was asleep by eleven. So Deeter took his pup tent, his sleeping bag, a jug of water, a flashlight, and a sack of potato chips, and went out back. He set up the tent, but he wasn't going to sleep in it. No way. He was sleeping in the shed with No-Name to make sure nothing happened to her.

"Move over," he said to the ugly chicken that came strutting out of her nesting box.

He closed the door behind him and unrolled his sleeping bag.

"I hope you don't snore," he said to No-Name.

Cluck, cluck, cluck. Cluck, cluck, cluck, went the chicken.

Deeter lay down on top of his sleeping bag and set his water and flashlight beside him. He ate eleven potato chips, saving the rest for breakfast, then stretched his arms and closed his eyes.

Cluck, cluck, cluck. Cluck, cluck, cluck, went the chicken, walking all around him. First the clucking went by his right ear. Then it traveled down his left side and came up the other.

Suddenly the chicken walked right up on Deeter's chest and crossed over, as though she were climbing a hill.

"For Pete's sake, settle down," he told her. "Don't you ever sleep?"

Cluck, cluck-a-cut, the hen said in answer, and Deeter didn't know what happened next because shortly after that he fell asleep.

At some point in the night the fox must have come around, because the chicken began to squawk. Deeter rolled over and sleepily turned on the flashlight. The door was still shut, and the chicken was safe, but there were soft noises from outside—a shuffling, scuffling, snuffing sort of sound. Deeter was too tired to get up and see what it was. He just banged on the side of the shed with the flashlight, and the noise went away.

In the morning Deeter opened his eyes and looked slowly about the shed. Had he only dreamed it, or had a fox come around in the night?

His eye fell on the shed door. Still closed.

He looked for the cockeyed chicken. Still there.

Smiling with relief, Deeter lay quietly a few minutes longer, then sat up. He felt something roll off his chest. *Crack. Crunch.*

An egg.

When Cornelia, Charles, and Mindy got to the shed the next morning, Deeter was hard at work on an old umbrella that had no handle. He was sitting on the floor with the opened umbrella upside down in his lap, trying to mount a fish mobile onto the metal shaft.

"What are you *doing?*" Cornelia said, crouching down beside him, and looking at the things he had collected. The cockeyed chicken who had been clucking in one corner, cocked her head and stared at the new arrivals, holding one foot in the air.

Deeter grinned. "It's almost done," he said. "Watch." Placing the upside-down umbrella in the middle of the floor, he gave it a spin and it went whirling around. The fishes hanging from the mobile swung back and forth as though they were swimming.

"So?" said Cornelia.

Deeter only smiled. He picked up a hammer and a six-inch nail and pounded it into the dirt floor through a dime-size hole near the center of the umbrella. Then he reached over for No-Name, put her in his lap, and with a short piece of ribbon, gently tied one end to the chicken's leg, the other end to the silky edge of the umbrella.

Charles began to grin.

"Is it going to hurt her?" Mindy asked.

"Not a bit," said Deeter. "Now. The test."

Setting the hen back on the ground and taking a handful of grain, he carefully placed the kernels about three inches apart in a wide circle around the umbrella. As No-Name moved forward, pecking at the grain, her foot turned the umbrella which rotated around the nail, and the little fishes began to sway and swim.

"Perfect!" cried Cornelia. "A chicken circus!" They watched some more as No-Name started and stopped, started and stopped—the fishes jerking this way and that. "Now all she needs is a costume," Cornelia added. "I'll have to find one for her."

"I think she needs some music" said Charles. "I've got an old music box. I could play along with her."

"What will I do?" asked Mindy, realizing that everyone else had made a contribution.

"Why don't you do that chicken dance you learned in camp last summer while Charles makes the music?" Cornelia suggested.

"This one?" said Mindy. She tucked her hands under her arms, flapped her elbows up and down, clucked like a chicken, and strutted round the shed, poking her head in and out, and making them all laugh.

"Perfect!" Cornelia said again.

They spent the afternoon helping No-Name get used to the ribbon around her leg, and watching Cornelia try out various doll clothes on the chicken, till finally they voted for a little red cape and a yellow straw hat that would have tied under the chin if chickens had chins.

"Now she's our present too," Cornelia said, as they put things away, carefully removing the fish mobile from the shaft of the umbrella, then folding the umbrella up and placing it in the cooler along with the costume and the music box and the chicken feed.

"Dad's *really* going to be surprised when he sees how well we've trained No-Name," said Charles.

"Here's the deal now," Cornelia went on. "After we have dinner on Friday, I'll come over and get the chicken, and the rest of you bring the other stuff."

"When do we eat the cake?" asked Charles.

"If all goes well, Charles, we'll get not only cake, but Starlight Park as well," Cornelia told him. "*If* everything goes well."

At that moment the one little window in the shed seemed to darken, and when Cornelia looked up, she thought she saw a face. Deeter, however, scrambled to his feet, but by the time he got to the door and opened it, there was only the sound of footsteps running among the trees.

$\infty8\infty$

The Following Night

Monday night, it was Charles's turn to sleep in the shed. He had received permission to spend the night at the Delaneys'. "We've got a sort of a camp back there, with a tent and everything," he had told his mother.

"Now *that's* the kind of thing that summer is for," said his mom. "The great outdoors!"

When it was time to go, he thrust a few things in his backpack and yelled, "I'm leaving now, Mom."

"Did you take a bath?" his mother called up the stairs.

"Yeah. Well . . ." he said, and lowered his voice. "Sort of."

"Did you put on a clean T-shirt?" the voice came again.

For Pete's sake! Charles wanted to bellow. *I'm sleeping with a chicken!* "Yeah," he said again.

"Be sure to thank Mrs. Delaney tomorrow for breakfast," Mother said.

"Good luck," whispered Cornelia as Charles left the house, his pack thrown over one shoulder.

Deeter came out to the shed to keep Charles company until it got dark; they took turns holding a flashlight under their chins and making horrible faces. No-Name appeared to be asleep, but every time Charles turned the light on her, one pink eye opened and the black pupil stared at Charles. Then the membrane closed again and the head began to nod.

"Dee-*ter!*" came Mrs. Delaney's voice finally.

"Gotta go," said Deeter. "And listen: If a fox tries to get in, throw red pepper in its face." He gave Charles a little bag of his mother's chili powder.

When the shed door closed again, Charles sat on his sleeping bag in one corner of the shed, back against the wall, and watched the chicken in the beam of his flashlight. Was this the stupidest thing he had ever done, or what? Man, oh, man, Starlight Park had better be worth all the work he was doing to get there. He wished he had eaten more dinner, because he didn't feel very full. He tried to put his mind on the rides at the amusement park, but his thoughts kept stopping at all the concession stands: cotton candy, strawberry smoothies, funnel cakes, foot-long hot dogs, popcorn, caramels . . .

He wondered what he *would* do if that old fox came sniffing and snuffing around. Maybe if he heard it digging away outside the shed, he'd wait until it stuck its head through the hole under the wall, and *then* he'd blast it with pepper.

Charles had brought a bunch of comic books, but was afraid if he used his flashlight any more he'd wear out the battery. He just might need that light later. So he climbed in his sleeping bag, turned over on his side, and prepared to go to sleep.

Perhaps he did sleep for a while, because when he first lay down he was lying on his left side, and when he woke he was lying on his back. He was too warm, for one thing, and thought about climbing out of the bag and lying on top, but he was too sleepy to actually do it.

Something else was wrong, however. There was definitely a noise from somewhere beyond the wall of the shed—a soft noise, a footstep kind of noise—a footstep or pawstep, perhaps, of a fox. A hungry fox. A fox who would come all the way out of the woods for a tender, plump chicken that was *supposed* to be a birthday present for somebody's mother.

Suddenly, before Charles could reach for his flashlight—the chili powder, even—the door of the shed swung open, there was a beam of light, and Charles found his sleeping bag rolling over and over with him inside it, his face in the dirt. And when the rolling stopped at last and he worked his way out of the bag, the shed was as quiet as a churchyard.

Charles crawled around until he found the flashlight against the wall. He turned it on. The shed was empty.

There was no fox; no chicken, either.

How could this be? What kind of fox could roll a boy over and over in his sleeping bag before he ran off with a chicken? Then Charles remembered the light. That was no fox!

He jumped up and dashed outside, looking this way and that. He ran down the path into the woods and looked around, hoping to see the beam of the chicken-robber's flashlight, but all was dark. He ran back the other way, into the Delaneys' yard. No beam of a flashlight there either.

Not again! Why did this have to happen on the night *he* was supposed to be guarding the chicken? Wasn't it enough that he had forgotten to latch the door once and the chicken had escaped? Now Deeter and Cornelia would *really* be mad, but what was he supposed to do?

Charles took it out on a tree, that's what he did. After knocking his head against the trunk, he kicked it once, kicked it twice, then grabbed one of the branches and shook it so hard that an owl, from somewhere above, hooted at him.

There was nothing left to do but go home and tell Cornelia what had happened. He didn't know what he would tell his mother when he rang the doorbell for her to let him in. Maybe he'd say he wasn't feeling well and decided to come back home. That was the truth. Charles was feeling terrible. No matter what he did, it turned out wrong. He wouldn't mind if his chickens did all come home to roost—one particular chicken, anyway.

He went back in the shed to roll up his sleeping bag, and the beam from his flashlight fell on a sheet of paper he had not noticed before. On the paper was a large blue circle. Inside the circle there was a red circle, and inside the red circle was a green one. Inside the green circle was this message:

If you ever want your stupid chicken back, you can look inside Susan Slager's shirt.

The Scoates Gang

◦9◦

Ransom

Charles stared at the note in his hand. It didn't make one bit of sense. Who was Susan Slager, and why would she be walking around with their chicken inside her shirt?

He stuffed the note in his pocket and walked home with his sleeping bag under his arm.

"What are *you* doing home?" Mother asked, coming to the door in her pajamas. She looked at him closely. "Are you sick?"

"Yes," said Charles. He was sick, all right. Sick to his stomach. "I thought I'd better come home in case I throw up."

"Gracious!" said Mother. "I'll bet you boys sat around eating junk food."

"No, we didn't," said Charles. "I went right to bed."

"Right to bed! You *are* sick!" Mother told him. "Go on upstairs and I'll bring the Pepto-Bismol."

"I'm not *that* sick!" Charles said, but before he knew it, Mother was walking behind him with the big pink bottle and a minute later one horrible mouthful was sliding down his throat.

When he was sure that Mother was in bed, Charles crept down the hall to Cornelia's room and softly opened the door.

"Cornelia," he whispered through the darkness.

No answer.

"Cor-*ne*-lia!" he whispered again.

The bedsprings squeaked.

"What *is* it?" Cornelia said. She didn't sound very pleasant. Cornelia was *never* pleasant when you woke her up.

"Who's Susan Slager?" asked Charles.

"How should *I* know?" snarled Cornelia. "What are you doing home? You're supposed to be guarding No-Name."

Charles swallowed. "The chicken's gone, Cornelia. Susan Slager kidnapped it, and she's got it in her shirt."

Cornelia bolted upright and turned on her lamp. "Are you crazy?"

Charles miserably sat down on the edge of her bed and told her what had happened.

Cornelia's eyes, which had grown wide at first with the story of the shed door flying open, grew narrower and narrower as she listened to the rest of the story.

"*Somebody*," she said, tightening her jaw, "has been spying on us and knew that chicken was in the Delaneys' shed. I'll bet someone thought you were Deeter."

Charles began to feel a little better. If somebody had a grudge against Deeter, then losing the chicken again wasn't exactly *his* fault, was it?

"Go on to bed," said Cornelia. "I'll handle this."

Those were the most wonderful words Charles had heard in a long, long time.

The next day the Morgan children got up as usual. They ate their breakfast as usual and did their morning chores. But when it came time to feed the chicken, they went over to the Delaneys' shed and waited for Deeter. All except Mindy. Cornelia decided not to tell her what had happened. Not yet, anyway. Besides, Mindy had started collecting bugs for No-Name and spent her mornings happily adding ladybugs and ants and beetles to the menu. It gave her something to do.

Deeter came out at last. He was wearing a baseball cap that said *Chicago White Sox* and a T-shirt that read *Chicago Bears* and Michael Jordan high-tops under the baggiest pants Cornelia had ever seen. The pockets were almost down to his knees. He whistled as he came down the path to the shed, and every so often he leaped into the air and practiced a one-handed hook shot with an imaginary basketball, hanging onto his pants with his other hand so he wouldn't lose them.

As soon as he got to the shed, however, and saw that the door was open, he stopped in his tracks. And when he peeked inside and saw Charles sitting in one corner, his back against the wall, and Cornelia, with her arms folded across her chest, sitting in another, he swallowed.

"Who," Cornelia asked, "is Susan Slager?"

Deeter's head began to swim. What was happening to his life? First he had taken Homer Scoates's multi-colored pen and made some boys mad at him, then he'd added a chicken to his problems, and right this moment Cornelia Morgan, who had begun to interest him very much, was asking about a girl he hardly knew.

"What?" asked Deeter, because he couldn't think of anything else to say.

"Who is she?" Cornelia repeated.

Deeter stared. Cornelia must be jealous! He hardly even *knew* Susan Slager, but somehow Cornelia must have thought he liked her.

"And why would she put a chicken down her shirt?" asked Charles, glaring at him.

Deeter began to feel his world slowly tipping sideways.

"*What?*" he said again.

Charles showed him the note. *The Scoates Gang*, it said at the bottom.

Deeter swallowed. It was beginning to be clear. Very clear indeed. He had to stand here about as close to Cornelia as he would ever get, he imagined, and tell her about the stupid day at the stupid school when he had borrowed the stupid pen from Homer Scoates, and how, when he had dropped it from the top of the stupid monkey bars, it had fallen down the back of a stupid shirt, worn by a girl named Susan Slager. Now, it seemed, he was going to go on paying for it for the rest of his stupid life.

"See?" Charles said after he'd heard the story. "Your chickens are all coming home to roost!" Now Grandma's saying was beginning to make sense. And then, to Cornelia, "What are we going to *do?* Mom's birthday is only three days off."

"What we are going to do," she said, "is wait for another note."

"What other note?" asked Charles.

"A ransom note," said Cornelia.

○10○
Waiting for Homer

By five o'clock that afternoon, Mindy had caught two crickets, a ladybug, three beetles, a centipede, and a moth. Cornelia had to tell her that the chicken was gone.

Mindy threw up her hands with the open jar in one, scattering bugs to the four winds. "Okay, that's it!" she said. "No-Name's gone forever. Good-bye, birthday party! Good-bye, merry-go-round."

"Maybe not," said Cornelia. "Tonight *I'm* going to sleep in the shed, and I'll bet Homer Scoates will deliver a ransom note. Criminals always return to the scene of the crime."

If only she felt as confident as she sounded, Cornelia thought. For all she knew, the Scoates gang was enjoying a fried chicken dinner that very moment. Still, she had to admit, this was interesting. Nothing like this had ever happened in Iowa.

Now the problem was getting Mother to let her sleep outside.

"It sure is a nice night out," Cornelia said that evening as she helped with the dishes.

"Yes, it is," said Mother. "I can smell the sweet peas I planted this spring."

"I smell them too!" said Cornelia. "In fact, the air smells so good I'd love to sleep outside this evening. Could I? In our camp?"

"What do you kids have over there?" asked Mother. "Where would you put your sleeping bag?"

"Deeter has a pup tent. It just holds one, but I haven't had a turn yet. I'd love to sleep outside on the ground under the stars," said Cornelia. She didn't exactly say she wouldn't be in the tent, and she didn't mention that there would be a roof between her and the stars, but if Mother was worried about safety, Cornelia would be even safer in the shed.

"Well, I suppose you could," said Mother. "This is a quiet neighborhood. Nothing ever happens here."

Ha! thought Cornelia.

"In fact," said Mother, "it sounds like so much fun, maybe I'll come camping with you!"

Cornelia felt herself freeze. Her tongue wouldn't even move.

But then Mother said, "No, I'm sure Mindy wouldn't like sleeping outdoors. I'd better stay in the house with her," and Cornelia could breathe again.

About nine that night, Cornelia took her sleeping bag and the flashlight and went over to the Delaneys' shed. She also took the red pepper, in case anyone tried to roll *her* up in a sleeping bag. But she had no intention of sleeping. She sat on her sleeping bag, back to the wall, pepper in one hand, flashlight in the other, and waited for the ransom note to be delivered.

An hour went by. Then two. The Mickey Mouse watch on Cornelia's wrist gleamed in the dark. She was beginning to nod off when she heard a noise, and her heart began to pound.

Footsteps?

A pause.

A snuffling, shuffling noise just outside the walls of the shed.

And suddenly Cornelia's anger got the best of her. How *dare* anyone steal her mother's chicken! How dare anyone put her through all this worry just to go to Starlight Park! How dare anybody make Cornelia sit up half the night in a stuffy shed waiting for some dumb boy to deliver a ransom note!

Without waiting for the note to be slipped under the door, Cornelia silently rose from her sleeping bag, inched her way across the floor, and flung open the door at the same instant she snapped on the flashlight.

There in the beam of light was a small red fox that stared at her for a moment, one paw off the ground, and in the next instant streaked off again and disappeared into the woods. Cornelia was so surprised that she forgot all about the red pepper.

She couldn't help laughing. If anybody has asked her on the last day of school what she would be doing a week from then, she never would have dreamed she would be spending the night with a chicken, outwitting a fox, and waiting for a ransom note. And all for the love of a roller coaster.

She closed the door of the shed again, lay down on top of her sleeping bag, and closed her eyes. A light rain began to fall on the roof of the shed—a gentle *pity-pat, pit pat, pity-pat, pit pat.*

Cornelia's breathing grew slower and deeper. Her eyes felt heavy, her legs went limp, and then she was dreaming that she was running down a long, long hill with a chicken cradled in her arms, a fox behind her, and the Scoates gang behind the fox.

When she opened her eyes, sunlight streamed through the one small window of the shed. Cornelia thought how delicious the sleeping bag felt beneath her, how refreshed she was feeling. She sat up slowly and looked around. And there, right as she had expected, was a note under the door of the shed.

She crawled over the dirt floor and picked it up.

Dear Stupid:
Susan Slager loves soup. If you don't want your dumb chicken turned into noodle soup, put five dollars in a Campbell's soup can and leave it

under the sickamore tree at the end of the play-
ground by four o'clock this afternoon.

The Scoates Gang

At the bottom of the paper was a blue circle. Inside the blue circle was a red one, and inside the red, a green one.

○11○

The Message and the Messenger

This was starting to get exciting. Cornelia went home with fire in her eyes. Because she was older than her brother and sister, she was allowed her own house key, so she quietly let herself in and went upstairs to her room.

Taking out a pen and a sheet of note paper, she carefully drew a skull and crossbones. Inside the skull, about where the eye sockets would be, she wrote:

> Give us proof that the chicken's alive or else!
> The Delaney-Morgan Mashers

"Mashers?" Charles asked, after Cornelia went in his room and showed him her note.

"I want us to sound tough," she said. *Two* days until Mother's birthday, and no chicken in sight.

The door to Charles's bedroom suddenly swung open, and there stood Mindy in her nightgown.

"Well, did No-Name come back or what?" she demanded.

"No," said Cornelia, "but we got a ransom note." Mindy listened solemnly while Cornelia explained about the first note Charles had found and about Susan Slager and the multicolored pen.

"Why does Susan Slager have No-Name in her shirt?" asked Mindy.

"She doesn't, of course. Homer is just trying to give Deeter some of his own medicine." Cornelia said. She turned to Charles. "But it might have *something* to do with a shirt. Maybe that's a clue—we should be looking for a shirt. Did the note say it was *in* her shirt or *down* her shirt or *wrapped* in a shirt, or what? Where's the *note?*"

Charles looked around his room. He got out of bed and searched the pockets of the jeans he'd been wearing the day before. "I don't know," he said. "I guess I lost it. It could be anywhere."

Cornelia was exasperated. "How could you *lose* it? You just had it yesterday. You didn't take it anywhere, did you?"

Charles swallowed. "After dinner last night," he confessed, "I took the note and rode over to the school playground asking kids if they knew Susan Slager. I thought maybe if I just told her myself how much we need that chicken back, she'd give it to me."

"You actually showed that note around?"

"Not exactly."

"Well, did you find her?"

"No. They said she wasn't there."

Cornelia sighed. "Well, you know where Homer Scoates lives, don't you?"

They all knew where Homer lived, because when Homer had chicken pox last spring and didn't have to go to school, he sat at the window of the big yellow house on the corner of Main and Locust and thumbed his nose at people as they went by.

"Yes, I know," said Charles.

"I want you to take this message to his house and deliver it *personally*. You have to *hand* it to him. Not his mother or dad or sister or cousin. Put it in Homer Scoates's own hand. Do you understand?"

"Yes," said Charles again, as she gave him the slip of paper. Cornelia sounded like the Queen of England. If the stupid note was so important, why didn't she deliver it herself?

But there was no refusing Cornelia, so Charles pulled on his clothes, stuffed the note in his jeans' pocket, and ten minutes later was on his way to Homer Scoates's house.

Homer lived about two blocks away. As Charles walked along the street, he counted all the newspapers that were lying on porches and realized that half the neighborhood was still asleep. In fact, Homer Scoates was probably still sleeping.

When Charles got to the Scoates's house, sure

enough, the blinds were drawn and the newspaper lay on the porch.

Charles stood looking at the house. In one of those rooms in one of those beds was an ordinary boy who was causing more trouble than anyone could possibly imagine. Homer was a year older than Charles but a year younger than Deeter and Cornelia. Charles wondered why Deeter didn't just punch Homer Scoates in the nose and get it over with.

He sighed. Resting on one foot, then the other, he finally sat down on the curb across from Homer's house, watching for any sign of life—a blind rising, a light going on, a door opening . . . Nothing.

When fifteen minutes had gone by, possibly twenty, and still nothing had happened, Charles crossed the street, went up on the Scoates's front porch, and peered in the picture window. Then he went around the house looking in one window after another. On the back porch he put his hand up to the glass and took a long look inside, but there was no mother baking biscuits, no father making pancakes, no children pouring cereal. Charles began to feel hungry. He went around to the front porch again, and this time, he had an idea. Lying on his stomach, he could see a thin crack under the door. If he could slip Cornelia's note through the crack, he could go home and have breakfast. Never mind that he was supposed to hand it to Homer. He was hungry!

Charles took the paper from his pocket and began pushing it under the door. It went partway, then stopped. There must be a mat or rug or something on the other side that kept it from going all the way in, Charles thought. He shoved and shoved, moving the paper this way and that.

All of a sudden he felt a tug. Someone had hold of the paper and was pulling it inside. Maybe it wasn't Homer, maybe it was his dad. And Charles began to think this was a bad idea after all. He held on tightly himself. The paper went one way, then another. Back and forth, back and forth.

Suddenly the door opened wide, and there was Homer Scoates down on his hands and knees.

"What do you want?" asked Homer, who was still in his pajamas. Dinosaur pajamas, with *Stegosauruses* all over the tops and bottoms, and a *Tyrannosaurus rex* on the shirt pocket.

"I'm supposed to give you this note from Cornelia," Charles told him.

"So why didn't she bring it herself?" Homer asked.

"I don't know," Charles told him. "I don't know anything anymore."

Homer read the note.

"Proof? She wants *proof?*" he said. "Just a minute."

He went back inside and returned with a white feather. "Give that to your sister." Then he reached out for the morning newspaper, pulled it inside, and shut the door.

Charles walked home with the feather in his pocket. Cornelia met him at the door.

"Well? Did you see the chicken?" she whispered.

"No, but Homer gave me this," said Charles, coming inside, and he pulled the white feather from his pocket.

Cornelia stared. "What does *that* prove?" she hissed. "That feather could have come from a dead chicken, for all we know. How do we know that No-Name hasn't already been eaten?"

Charles couldn't believe he had been so stupid. Cornelia was right. No-Name could have been stuffed and roasted by now.

There were footsteps on the stairs behind him, and Mother came down.

"Well, *you* two are up early this morning," she said. "I was thinking of making French toast." She had just reached the bottom step when the doorbell rang.

Cornelia opened the door. A policeman in a dark blue uniform seemed to be blocking the whole entrance.

"Good morning," he said, looking right at Charles. And then, to Cornelia, "I wonder if I could speak with your brother."

○12○
Deeter's Turn

"Charles?" said Mother, stepping forward as Mindy appeared at the top of the stairs. And then, to the officer, "You want to speak to my son? What on earth for?"

"Just a few questions, ma'am, that's all," said the policeman.

Charles took a deep breath and walked over to the screen door.

"Would you step outside, please?" the officer asked.

"No!" Mindy screamed and rushed down the stairs. "Don't take my brother to jail! Please don't take him to jail!" she shrieked, throwing herself at the policeman.

The officer looked startled. "Sweetheart, I'm not taking your brother anywhere. I just want to talk with him a minute."

Sobbing, Mindy stood with her nose pressed against the screen while Mother and Cornelia listened from a few feet away.

"Son, were you down at the corner of Main and Locust streets this morning?" the officer asked.

Charles scratched his neck. "Yes."

"A neighbor reported seeing a boy about your age looking in the window of the Scoates's house. She said she watched while you went around to all the windows, and finally it looked as though you were trying to pry open the front door. That's when she called the police."

"I wasn't trying to open the door," Charles told him. "I was trying to push a note underneath, and I didn't knock because I was afraid I'd wake someone up."

"I see," said the policeman. "Well, I didn't figure you were trying to break in, but the lieutenant wanted me to check it out. I pulled up in front of their house in time to see you disappearing around the block, and followed you here. Next time, maybe you should go a little later when people are up and you can just ring the bell."

"Okay," said Charles. There would never be a next time if he could help it. He didn't care if he got to be ninety years old and had still not gone to Starlight Park, he would never go near Homer Scoates's house again.

The policeman tipped his cap to Mother and went down the steps to the squad car.

"Good-bye! Have a nice day!" Mindy called happily.

"All right!" said Mother, her arms folded across her chest. "Now what?"

The phone rang and Charles, Cornelia, and Mindy

could hear the caller's voice. "Helen, is anything wrong at your house?" asked Mrs. Hoover.

"Yes, but nothing that a week of kitchen duty won't cure," said Mother. And after she hung up, she said, "First you saw all the bristles off my new broom, and now a policeman follows you home. What am I going to do with you, Charles? Why *were* you on the Scoates's front porch this morning?"

"It's my fault!" said Cornelia quickly. "I asked him to deliver a note to Homer Scoates. I didn't realize it would cause so much trouble. He shouldn't have to do the dishes alone. We'll both do them."

"Cornelia, you shouldn't be writing notes to boys in the first place," Mother scolded. "If you have a boyfriend, invite him here."

"A *boyfriend?*" Cornelia gagged. And Charles heard her mutter, "Just wait till I get my hands on Deeter."

She didn't have long to wait, because she and Charles and Mindy had just finished their cereal and were sitting on the back steps sorting clothes from the laundry basket when Deeter sauntered out the back door of his house, eating a piece of toast. The pair of pants he wore hung so low that Charles didn't see how they stayed up at all.

Cornelia fairly flew across the yard until she was out of earshot of her house. At first Deeter had the wild notion that she was going to throw her arms around his neck and tell him that No-Name was back. Instead, she put her hands on his shoulders and shook him hard.

"Deeter Delaney!" she hissed. "It's only two more days till Mother's birthday, and we need that chicken back! If you hadn't taken Homer Scoates's pen, No-Name would still be safe in the shed."

Deeter dropped his toast and stumbled backward, holding onto the top of his trousers.

Cornelia told him about the note she'd found in the shed that morning and how Charles had gone to Homer's with her reply and come home with a policeman behind him.

"That feather doesn't prove a thing, and we are not paying a ransom of five dollars for a chicken that might be potpie already," she declared.

Deeter drew himself up as tall as he could. "I'll go," he said. "I'll go see Homer myself. And I'll either come back with proof that No-Name's alive, or I'll bring the chicken with me."

Cornelia's eyes softened and she gave him a grateful smile.

Deeter went back home and brushed his teeth. Then he sat down and thought about what he was going to say. He ate another piece of toast and brushed his teeth again.

Well, he told himself finally, *there are more of them than there are of me, but the worst that can happen is*

that they'll break my nose and beat me black and blue.
Did he really want to go to Starlight Park? he wondered. Was it worth all this to ride the Mad Hornet and the Whirl-o-Wheel? Yes, he decided, because what else was there to do this summer? He couldn't hide out here for three whole months waiting for the feud between him and the Scoates gang to blow over, especially since the gang had taken to spying on him from the woods. A whole week had gone by and he hadn't shot one single solitary basket.

So he set off down the street, rounded the corner, and walked toward the big yellow house.

There on the steps sat Homer Scoates, surrounded by all six members of his gang. They were all scowling and looking as fierce as pit bulls. When they saw Deeter, however, they began to laugh.

"That is some ugly chicken!" sang out Homer.

"Yeah," said one of his buddies. "If that chicken was any uglier, they'd put it in a freak show."

"Uglier than ugly," said another.

"That chicken is so ugly that if you put it in soup, no one would eat it," said a third.

Deeter bravely planted himself on the sidewalk. He was doing this for Cornelia. "You have a choice," he told them. "Either you give me real proof that the chicken's alive, in which case we will *consider* paying the five bucks, or we will break into your house, steal the chicken, and you won't get anything at all."

"Ha! Just try it!" said Homer, and he and his buddies laughed.

"Then how about if the Delaney-Morgan Mashers meet you at the playground and punch out your lights?" said Deeter.

"Ha!" said Homer again, but nevertheless, he and his buddies huddled together whispering.

"Okay," Homer said at last. He went inside and finally came back with his fingers cupped in front of him. "Hold out your hands."

Deeter did as he was told, and Homer emptied his hands over Deeter's. Plop. A round green blob of chicken poop. And it was still warm.

13

Rescue

By the time Deeter realized what he had in his hands, Homer and his gang had scrambled up the steps and locked themselves behind the screen door. They were making faces at him and yelling:

"Dee-ter!
Dee-ter!
Couldn't hurt a
'skeet-er!"

As they sang, they stuck their thumbs on their noses and waggled their fingers.

"I want that chicken, and you'd better have it ready!" Deeter yelled back.

"Four o'clock at the sycamore tree," Homer croaked delightedly, "with five dollars in a Campbell's soup can."

"Nobody gets that money until we see the chicken, alive and well," said Deeter.

"You'll see it. Just be there," sang out Homer, and all the gang members waggled their fingers once again.

It was humiliating. *Why* had he teased Homer

Scoates in the first place? Deeter asked himself. *Why had he taken his multicolored pen?*

Deeter went home and called Cornelia.

"I've got two dollars and fifteen cents," he said. "How much do you have?"

"About three dollars, and Charles has a quarter," she answered. "Mindy doesn't have any money at all."

"Okay, I'll get the soup can. We'll all go to the sycamore tree together," Deeter said

At four o'clock that afternoon, not a minute sooner, not a minute later, Cornelia, Charles, Mindy, and Deeter, carrying an empty tomato soup can, walked three blocks to the school. There were a few kids playing on the swings, one on the slide, two on the merry-go-round, and a bunch of boys shooting baskets.

Far off in a corner of the playground stood the old sycamore tree.

"Do they really think we're just going to put five dollars in a can and walk away?" asked Cornelia. "Why, anyone could come along and take it."

"We're not going to walk away. We're going to stay right there until someone shows up with the chicken," Deeter told her.

The corner of the playground where the sycamore stood seemed to be deserted. There was no sign of a boy or chicken anywhere.

"I'll bet this is just a trick to get the five dollars,"

said Charles. "They shouldn't get five dollars. They should get a punch in the face."

"Do you want to start the fight?" Deeter asked him. "There are seven boys in the Scoates gang. You and Cornelia and I would each have to take on two apiece, and there's even one of them left over to get Mindy." Charles swallowed again. He'd been doing a lot of swallowing lately.

They walked up to the tree and stood looking in all directions.

"Just lay it on the ground," said a voice from the tree, and Deeter looked up to see fourteen legs swinging from two large branches above them.

"Don't do it, Deeter!" said Cornelia. "Not until we have the chicken."

Squawk! came a loud noise above them, and a mesh laundry bag was slowly lowered on a rope until it dangled about three feet above their heads. In the bag was No-Name, her toes sticking out the tiny holes in the bottom.

"Okay," Cornelia told Deeter. They dropped their money inside the can. "Put the can by the tree."

"No, throw it up to us," said Homer, swinging his legs and grinning. "Throw it to us instead."

"How do we know we'll get the chicken?" asked Deeter.

"The minute we catch the can, we'll drop the rope," said one of Homer's friends.

Deeter swung back his arm and made an under-handed throw to the boys in the tree, while Cornelia and Charles raised their arms to catch No-Name. But the bag did not fall. The minute Homer Scoates had the Campbell's soup can with the five dollars in it, he jerked on the rope, and the bag zoomed back up in the air with another loud squawk from the cockeyed chicken.

"Hey!" yelled Charles.

"Give us that chicken!" Cornelia demanded.

"We want to see you beg! We want to see you *crawl!*" chortled Homer, obviously enjoying himself. "Get down on your hands and knees and crawl around the tree three times, and then we'll lower your dumb chicken."

The demand sounded all too familiar to Deeter.

"No way!" cried Cornelia. "You give us that chicken or else!"

"Or else what?" The Scoates gang laughed, and swung their legs all the harder.

At that moment, however, one of the boys stopped swinging and stared across the playground. Then another boy stopped swinging his legs, and another and another.

Cornelia looked where the boys were staring. Then Charles and Deeter and Mindy turned. Coming across the playground toward them was a large girl with arms like rolling pins and a face as fierce as Cornelia had ever seen. She was wearing army camouflage shorts and a brown T-shirt with the words, *Don't mess with me,* on the front. She was also wearing knee pads and holding a hockey stick.

"Who's *that?*" Cornelia asked.

And the Homer Scoates gang answered, "Susan Slager!"

◯14◯
Plans

Susan Slager was the toughest-looking girl Deeter Delaney had ever seen. She didn't need a message on her T-shirt. Nobody would mess with her, no matter what. She looked as though she could hide not only a chicken under her shirt, she could hide a whole coop full of chickens!

He had never been this close to her, actually. He had never been this close to any of the sixth-grade girls, and he could feel her breath on his face when she stomped up to where they were standing.

Susan Slager put her hands on her hips and looked around at Deeter, Cornelia, and Charles. She didn't even bother with Mindy.

"Where," she boomed, and her voice sounded like gravel going down a tin chute, "will I find Homer Scoates and his gang?"

Cornelia, Charles, and Deeter raised their hands at the same time and pointed up the tree.

Seven pairs of legs dangled motionless from the limbs above. Seven pairs of eyes stared fearfully down at the big girl with the hockey stick.

Susan Slager reached into the pocket of her army camouflage shorts and pulled out a piece of paper.

"*If you ever want your stupid chicken back, you can look inside Susan Slager's shirt,*" she read aloud.

"Who wrote this?"

All six of Homer Scoates's so-called friends pointed their fingers at him.

Charles realized that when he was riding around the playground looking for Susan Slager, he must have dropped the note, and somehow it got to Susan.

"*Nobody* looks inside my shirt," said Susan and, dropping her hockey stick on the ground, she began to climb the tree.

Like rats deserting a ship, boys began jumping from the sycamore—tumbling, diving, leaping, yelping. They landed on knees and elbows, on hands and bottoms, but no sooner did each boy hit the ground than he scrabbled to his feet again and ran as fast as the wind. In all the commotion, Homer dropped the rope, and, with wings flapping inside the laundry bag, the chicken fluttered to the ground.

Cornelia, Charles, Mindy, and Deeter didn't look back. Holding their precious chicken in their arms, they ran all the way home and didn't stop till they were safely inside the Delaneys' shed.

Cornelia leaned against one wall and closed her eyes, panting until she caught her breath. She couldn't help laughing, however. "What a debacle this turned out to be!" she said, remembering another word on her advanced spelling list.

"A what?" asked Charles.

"A mess. A mix-up. A disaster. A joke. The Great Chicken Debacle, that's what this is. Oh, Deeter, did you see the looks on their faces when Susan Slager started up that tree?"

"Did you see how fast they bailed out?" hooted Charles.

"Well, we've got No-Name back," said Deeter, and then, turning to the chicken who was making her way out of the laundry bag, he said, "Hey, you. Are you worth all this trouble? Huh?"

No-Name fluffed her feathers indignantly, spread her wings, and clucked loudly.

Suddenly Cornelia stopped laughing. "The can! Homer still has our five dollars!"

Deeter let out a low moan.

But Mindy triumphantly held the can up in the air, the five dollars safe inside. "They dropped it," she said.

"Hey, Mindy! Way to go!" shouted Deeter.

"Good *girl!*" said Charles, suddenly proud of his little sister, and Mindy's smile spread from ear to ear.

But Cornelia took charge once more. "Okay, someone has to stay with No-Name every single minute until Mother's birthday on Friday. We can't leave this chicken for one second."

"I'll do it," said Deeter quickly, wanting Cornelia to see how dependable he could be. "I'll stay on watch all night long, and protect this chicken with my life."

"Promise?" asked Cornelia.

"Promise," said Deeter.

The next morning when the Morgan children went to Deeter's, making their way through the lawn chairs they had dragged back there, around the pup tent and the big blue cooler where he kept the chicken feed, the music box, and the umbrella contraption, plus some Gatorade, they could hear a steady thunk, thunk, thunk coming from somewhere. They weren't sure where. It wasn't coming from inside the shed, and when they opened the door, they saw No-Name dozing peacefully in her box. So they closed the door and looked around.

Back by the creek, on the path to the road, Deeter was hard at work with a shovel. They could see nothing below his knees, however, because he was standing in a hole.

"What are you *doing?*" Cornelia asked.

"Don't worry. I can see the shed from here. If anyone came along to take No-Name, I'd nab him," Deeter assured her.

"What's with the ditch?" Charles wanted to know, when he saw that the hole was at least four feet long.

"It's not just a ditch," Deeter said, lowering his

voice in case there were spies about. "Which way do you think Homer Scoates came from when he stole No-Name?"

"This way, of course," said Cornelia, pointing toward the road. "I doubt he'd walk right through our yards."

"Exactly," said Deeter. "So if his gang comes back, at least one of them will fall in my booby trap." Sweat dripped down the sides of his face and his shirt was damp. It was too hot a morning to be digging a ditch, and he had obviously been at it for a long time already.

Mindy studied it skeptically. "Maybe they'll just walk around," she said.

"Not if they come after dark," said Deeter. "And not if we cover it with sticks and leaves."

"But Deeter!" Cornelia said. "Even if somebody does fall in, he'll just crawl out again. How deep are you going to make it?"

"That's not the point," Deeter told her. "The point is to make it just deep enough that if anyone tumbles in, he'll yell. And if he yells, I'll hear him. At least I'll be ready."

It seemed like a good enough idea that Cornelia got Dad's shovel from the garage, and she and Charles took turns digging too. They had never in their lives made a booby trap! Even if there were no Homer Scoates, it might be fun to make a trap, just to see what would happen. When the ditch across the path was about three feet deep, they decided that was deep enough.

While Mindy sat in a lawn chair outside the shed, making sure no one came by to steal the chicken, Deeter and Cornelia and Charles worked to weave twigs and leaves across the opening of the ditch and covered the pile of dirt as well. It would have been hard for anyone to know there was a three foot deep hole beneath.

The day dragged on. It grew hotter and hotter, muggier and muggier.

"Whew!' said Mother, when the three Morgan children went home for lunch. "I thought we'd eat out on the back porch, but it's just too hot. A storm is supposed to roll in tomorrow. I surely hope so."

"Not on your birthday!" said Charles.

"Oh, we'll have fun, no matter what," Mother said. "I *love* a good storm, the louder the better."

That afternoon the children could think of nothing better to do than to put on their swimsuits and have a water fight. Out came water pistols, water balloons, towels soaked in water, then rolled up, and lobbed toward the nearest victim. They chased each other through their camp, around Deeter's tent, around the lawn chairs, hiding behind the shed and leaping out for an ambush, shrieking and yelping.

"That's for stealing Homer's pen!" Cornelia hollered as she squirted Deeter on the back of the neck.

"That's for being so bossy!" Charles yelled as he lobbed a wet towel at Cornelia's stomach.

"That's for leaving the shed door open!" Deeter brayed as he threw a water balloon at Charles but got Mindy instead and had to let her squirt him in the face to get even.

At one point Deeter picked up a whole pail of water and took off after Charles, around the shed, through the walnut trees, around the lawn chairs, leaping over the creek and back again, and then it happened: *ker-thwack!* Charles disappeared.

"Charles?" cried Cornelia.

"It works!" yelled Deeter. "The booby trap works."

From the depths of the ditch, however, came a howl of pain. Cornelia and Deeter and Mindy ran over to see Charles half lying in the ditch, holding his ankle, his face twisted in a grimace. He howled again as Deeter and Cornelia pulled him out and helped him over to a lawn chair.

"Shhhh," Cornelia kept saying. "Shhhh, Charles. Keep it down."

Too late. Mother was already coming through the walnut trees toward camp.

No-Name, don't cluck! Cornelia pleaded silently as Mother stopped right outside the shed, looking about, and then hurried over to Charles who was holding his foot in his hands.

"What happened? Did you fall?" said Mother.

"It . . . it's nothing," Charles grimaced.

But now Mrs. Delaney had heard the commotion and was coming around the bushes from the house.

"He didn't fall out of a tree, did he?" she asked. "You kids aren't playing chicken again, are you?"

Mindy looked wide-eyed at Cornelia. And when no one said a word, she took it upon herself to explain: "He fell in a booby."

"A *what?*" Mrs. Delaney said.

"A booby," Mindy said again, looking hesitantly at her sister.

"Where did he fall, Mindy?" asked Mother.

Mindy pointed, and Mother and Mrs. Delaney walked back to the path near the creek.

"Who in the world dug this ditch? It's downright dangerous!" said Deeter's mom. And then her eye fell on two shovels, hers and the Morgans'. "Deeter, did you dig this hole?" she asked.

"We all did," said Cornelia quickly. "We were just protecting our camp."

"Well, what in the world is so important back here that you have to booby-trap the place?" Mother demanded. "If the Hoovers decided to take a stroll after dinner or the mailman cut through here on his way to the next block, we could have people breaking their legs right and left. Cornelia, you take that shovel and start putting the dirt back in this minute."

"B . . . but . . . ," Cornelia protested.

"*Now!*" said her mother.

"Deeter?" said Mrs. Delaney, and didn't have to say another word because Deeter had already begun to shovel beside Cornelia.

"Charles, can you walk on that foot at all?" Mother asked.

"I . . . I think so," he said as she examined it carefully.

"Well, I don't think there are any broken bones, but we need to get some ice on it. Your dad's coming home from Peoria tonight, and you kids better get cleaned up. But Cornelia's going to stay until that ditch is filled."

Charles cast an apologetic glance at his sister and Deeter, and then, limping along beside his mother with Mindy in the rear, started for home.

A half hour later Cornelia came in, ready for a bath.

"Don't worry," she whispered to Charles. "Deeter's staying out in the shed again tonight. And by tomorrow at this time, it will all be over, we hope."

Father got home about five-thirty and studied the kids' faces. "Well," he said, his eyes twinkling as he set his sample case on the floor. "Are we all ready for your mother's birthday? Everything ready to go?"

"Absolutely," said Cornelia.

"Positively," said Charles.

"I guess," said Mindy.

Mother laughed as she kissed her husband on the cheek. "Sounds to me as though you guys have a surprise cooked up for tomorrow."

"We didn't *cook* it!" Mindy said.

"*Mindy!*" cried Cornelia and Charles together.

Mindy looked chagrined. "I didn't say . . ."

"*Shut up!*" yelped Charles, and Cornelia immediately clapped her hand over Mindy's mouth.

Father laughed. "Come on. I'm starving. Let's eat," he said, but he gave the kids a thumbs-up as they followed Mother to the kitchen.

Before she went to bed that night, Cornelia crept over to the shed and tapped lightly on the door.

The door opened slowly, and suddenly Cornelia was confronted by a hideous creature, with a slimy green face and fangs. She gave a little shriek before she realized it was holding a flashlight in one hand and a baseball bat in the other.

"Deeter!" she scolded.

The creature laughed, and Deeter removed a latex Halloween mask from his face. "Anybody tries to get in *here* tonight, he's got a surprise coming," Deeter said. "What do you want?"

"I just wanted to be sure everything's okay," Cornelia told him.

"Everything's okay," he said. The shed, however,

looked as though it were slowly becoming his bedroom. There was not only a sleeping bag, but a pillow. On top of the cooler that Deeter was now using for a bedside table were magazines, potato chips, popcorn, a water jug . . . . It looked almost cozy, if it hadn't been so warm in the shed. No-Name didn't seem to mind, however, and was comfortably nesting in the box they had made for her.

"Can you honestly stay awake all night if you have to?" asked Cornelia.

"I'm sure going to try," said Deeter.

"Okay. If you can make it through tonight, Deeter, you'll never have to sleep out here again," Cornelia told him.

She went back across the wet grass to her own house. The air was still warm and humid, and she wondered how Deeter could stand being in that shed all night with the door closed. The tent would be a lot more comfortable, but they couldn't take that chance.

Even though everything seemed okay, even though Deeter said he would stay awake, even though the cockeyed chicken herself was nodding peacefully in her nesting box when Cornelia last checked, she had the awful, terrible feeling that an awful, terrible something was about to happen.

○15○

The Awful, Terrible Something

When Cornelia woke the next morning, it was warmer still. Instead of cooling things off, the night seemed to have made the air even stickier. It was hot, it was humid, and not at all pleasant in the shed, she knew. But in about ten more hours they would be celebrating Mother's birthday, the secret would be out, and then she could put her mind on the Screaming Cyclone and the rest of summer.

She had thought she wanted to ride in the very first car with her hands up over her head, but maybe it would be more fun riding in the very last seat. She tried to imagine how she felt on a roller coaster when it whipped around a corner, jerking her to one side, then whipped the other way. How it raced around a curve, clanked along to the top of a rise, and then plunged, everyone screaming, down the other side.

Did she want to sit alone or would she go with Deeter? If she didn't sit with him, the attendant might put someone else in beside her, someone who would cry or grab hold of her arm or something. She'd better ride with Deeter. Maybe they could buy ten tickets and ride five times in the first car and five times in the last, just to see what was scariest.

She pulled on the same shorts and tank top she had worn the day before, then remembered it was Mother's birthday and chose a green and yellow set. She even brushed her hair and put a white and yellow scrunchie around her ponytail.

Her father was just leaving for the office when she came downstairs.

"If it rains this afternoon, it will probably break the heat," he said, and then he whispered, "We'll give Mother our gifts right after dinner, okay? Everything all set?"

"We're ready!" Cornelia said.

He winked. "Good job!" he said. "*Very* good job! I never thought you could do it."

It was wonderful to see that the night had passed without anything happening to the chicken. All morning the children practiced for the evening's performance. Mindy did her chicken dance while Charles, his ankle in an Ace bandage, turned the little crank on the music box. Cornelia took a brown grocery sack and made a chicken headdress for Mindy to wear while she danced. The only one they didn't let practice was No-Name, because they wanted her to be hungry when it was time for her act.

After lunch, while Deeter remained in the camp, Cornelia, Charles, and Mindy tried to be as helpful as possible at home. Cornelia made the beds, Charles took out the garbage, and Mindy cleaned her fingernails.

They slipped over to the shed one more time to make sure that No-Name was safe and to give Deeter a rest break. He came back to the shed in a fresh T-shirt and pants that looked as though they had stretched with each wearing. If they hung any lower, Cornelia thought, he could use them for boots.

"You and your mom are invited to the party after dinner," Cornelia told him. "We should be through about seven, and we want you to come over for ice cream and cake. I'll help you bring the chicken and all our stuff."

"Boy, I wish the party was right now. I wish we didn't have to worry about this chicken one more minute!" said Charles.

"So do I," said Cornelia. "Do you realize we haven't been to the pool or a movie once since school was out? But it's been fun . . . sort of. Right now I have to go home and make a birthday cake. Mom's going to the beauty parlor, and I want to surprise her when she gets back."

"I'll sit over here with Deeter," said Charles.

"You will not! You've got to put up the decorations, and Mindy's got to set the table. I can't do everything myself," Cornelia said. She turned to Deeter. "We'll see you tonight. *Thank* you, Deeter! And *please* don't let anything happen to No-Name."

"I'm not letting this chicken out of my sight," Deeter told her.

At home, Mother glanced out the window before she left, and took her umbrella from the closet. "I hope I get back before it pours," she said. "That's the recipe for rain, all right. Either wash the car or get a perm, and it rains."

When her car was out of the driveway, the three children flew about getting things ready. Cornelia put the best cloth on the table, then left it for Charles and Mindy to set with the good china dishes while she prepared the cake mix and got it in the oven.

While the cake was cooling, they got out the box of party decorations and began twisting the long crepe paper streamers, taping them from the light fixture to the walls.

When the cake had been frosted, Cornelia, Charles, and Mindy all stood at the counter licking the bowl.

"Look how dark the sky's getting," Charles said, pointing out the window.

Cornelia stepped out onto the back porch. It wasn't any cooler, but a breeze had picked up and it felt delicious on her arms and legs. It wasn't long before the breeze became a wind, and then a light rain began to fall.

"If Mom doesn't get back soon, she's really going to get wet," Cornelia mused, as they hurriedly washed the dishes.

A car door slammed just then and Mother came through the front door.

"Cornelia? Charles?" she called. "There aren't any windows open, are there? I think we're in for a real storm."

"We'll check," Cornelia told her and ran upstairs as the rain began coming down in torrents. When all the windows were checked, Cornelia stood out on the back porch with Charles and Mindy, watching hail bounce off the porch steps.

"What do you think that sounds like in the shed?" Charles wondered. "Deeter must think there's a machine gun on the roof."

"Just so it doesn't upset No-Name," said Cornelia.

"Dee-ter!" called Mrs. Delaney from next door. "Dee-ter! Come inside."

At that moment another car door slammed, and there were heavy footsteps on the gravel driveway. The front door slammed next, and from inside the house, Father yelled, "Helen! Cornelia! I think we'd better get to the basement. Get Charles and Mindy, and hurry!"

The next thing Charles knew, his dad had him by the arm and was steering him through the back door and toward the basement. He collided with Mindy and felt Cornelia's knee bump his back as she and Mother hurried down the stairs behind him.

"Is it a tornado?" he asked.

"I don't know, but that wind is like nothing I ever felt before," Father said.

Mindy began to cry.

"We're okay, sweetheart," her father said. "I was listening to the news on the way home, and there's a tornado watch on for the area. It doesn't mean there is one—it just means that conditions are right for one. All this hot air meeting a cold front."

They usually couldn't hear the wind when they were in the basement, but this time they could.

"Gracious!" said Mother, sitting down on the floor while Mindy crawled onto her lap. "A birthday storm! Isn't *this* exciting!"

Cornelia knew from experience that when something bad was about to happen, Mother tried to make an adventure out of it. Booster shots from the doctor; a trip to the dentist—she always planned something nice to do on the way home. *Isn't this exciting?* just meant that Mother was scared too. From outside came the sound of breaking limbs and shutters banging.

"I hope we don't lose a tree," Father said.

They could hear the pelting of rain and the hail hitting the side of the house, striking the roof, and reverberating down the chimney.

"Well," said Mother. "At least the hot spell's over."

It seemed about seven or eight minutes before the hail gradually grew fainter, along with the wind. And finally there was just the light pit-a-pat of rain, and then even that stopped.

"Now! That wasn't so bad, was it?" Mother said to Mindy, getting to her feet.

They followed Father upstairs. When he opened the kitchen door, Cornelia held her breath, because she half expected to see the kitchen roof caved in, and the birthday cake and decorations in shambles.

Except for some leaves sticking to the window glass outside, however, everything was as they had left it, and the refrigerator was still humming. They opened the back door and stepped onto the porch. And then they gasped.

There was an old tree down in the Hoovers' back-yard and branches and twigs were strewn in every direction. Roots stuck up out of the ground, and Mr. and Mrs. Hoover themselves were coming down their back steps, shaking their heads.

"Well, at least it didn't hit the house," Mr. Hoover called over. "I just phoned the weather bureau, and they said there weren't any tornadoes touching down, but I told 'em if one didn't touch down in my back yard, it was the spittin' image of one—half a tornado, anyway."

But Father was staring out over their own yard. "Looks like it went right through here—you can see where some other trees are down back in the woods. And look there! We lost a limb off our beech tree."

But Cornelia and Charles were staring beyond the beech tree where they *should* have been able to see the roof of the Delaney's shed. All they could see was a tent draped over the high limb of a tree.

Cornelia grabbed Charles's arm. *Deeter!* The last she had seen of him, he was guarding the chicken. At that same moment they heard Mrs. Delaney frantically calling: "Deeter! Deeter!"

"Marjorie?" Father called. "Are you all right?"

"Yes, but where's Deeter?" Mrs. Delaney cried. "He never made it into the house. I hope he was with you!"

They all made their way across the limbs and branches toward the camp in the Delaneys' yard, but once it came into view, they stopped and stared. The chairs were overturned, the tent was up in a tree, and as for the shed, the roof was gone, one wall was gone, the door hung on a single hinge, and all around the entire yard—all over the soggy grass—were hundreds of little white feathers.

○16○
The Big Day

This was too much. Cornelia broke into tears. But Mrs. Delaney was frantic.

"Dee-ter!" she screamed, yanking up fallen tree branches as though her boy might be beneath one. "Deeter!"

"Deeter!" Father boomed.

It was Mindy, though, who saw him first.

"Deeter!" she cried, and everyone turned.

Deeter Delaney was crawling out from under his back porch, his face dirty, his hair disheveled, wearing only his shirt and underwear. His baggy pants had, one might say, gone with the wind.

But Deeter was too dazed to notice. His mother rushed over and swooped him close in her arms. When she realized at last that he was standing there in his underpants, she picked up the first thing she could find, a rain-soaked tablecloth which had been hanging on the clothesline, and wrapped it around him.

Cornelia was so glad to see Deeter—so happy she would not have to go her whole life remembering that

Deeter had given his life for a chicken—that she too rushed over and gave him a hug.

Deeter, who had been dazed before, stood absolutely stupefied now. When Cornelia whispered, "I'm sorry about No-Name, but I'm glad you're alive," however, he suddenly came to his senses.

"Where *is* she?" he whispered back. "I tried to save her, Cornelia, but the last I saw of her, she was flying through the air."

"Look," said Cornelia sadly, and pointed to the white feathers scattered all over the yard. Even if they found No-Name alive, she knew, the hen would look awful without her feathers. Out on the farm Grandma would say, "A chicken looking *that* bad is only good for the stew pot."

At that moment there was another noise, a familiar noise, a welcome noise—a gentle *cluck, cluck, cluck.* Across the cluttered yard came a cockeyed, crooked-legged, crusty-combed chicken, minus a feather or two.

Cornelia, Charles, Mindy, and Deeter all whirled around.

"No-Name!" cried Mindy.

"She's alive!" screamed Cornelia and Deeter.

"She's come back home to roost!" yelped Charles.

"Then what . . . ?" said Cornelia, staring at all the feathers.

"That's what was left of my pillow," said Deeter, and suddenly all four children began to laugh.

Father scooped the dirty white hen up in his arms and carried her over to Mother. "For you!" he said. "To remind you of the farm."

"*What?*" cried Mother, staring.

"Happy birthday!" said Father, laughing. And suddenly everyone was laughing.

"Oh, Tom!" Mother said. "You *would* think of something like this. Why . . . why, this is the goofiest-looking chicken I ever saw!" She threw back her head and laughed some more. "Where did you get her?"

"One of my customers was selling his poultry business and gave her to me last week," Father said.

"What? But . . . where have you been *keeping* her all this time?" asked Mother.

"Now that," said Father, "is a long story. I'll let Cornelia tell you."

"But not now," said Cornelia. "This isn't just a chicken, Mom, it's a *special* chicken." And while Deeter went inside for his trousers, Cornelia and Charles hurried to the shed, relieved to find the cooler still there.

As the grown-ups continued inspecting their yards, Cornelia and Charles, Mindy, and Deeter cleared a space in the walnut grove and brought out the things they would need for their show. When everything was ready, they called to their parents and all the adults came over, Mr. and Mrs. Hoover too.

"What's this?" asked Father.

"*Any*one can give a live chicken," Cornelia told him, "but this is a *performing* chicken!"

"You don't say!" said Father, surprised.

"Wonderful!" said Mother. "Let the show begin."

Mindy put on the chicken headdress as Charles began turning the handle on the music box. The cockeyed chicken, in a little red cape and a yellow hat, began to peck at the grain, the umbrella began to turn, the fishes began to swim, and Mindy started her famous chicken dance, flapping her elbows up and down, poking her neck in and out, and making little clucking noises in her throat.

"Why, that chicken ought to be in a circus!" said Mrs. Hoover.

"Living next door to these kids *is* a circus!" said Mr. Hoover.

Dum . . . dee . . . dum went the music box. *Peck . . . peck . . . peck* went the chicken. *Stomp . . . stomp . . . stomp* went Mindy, flapping her arms and dancing behind No-Name, as Cornelia and Deeter joined in, poking their heads in and out and hopping first on one foot, then the other, in time to the music.

Then Father joined in, flapping his arms up and down too and hopping about the circle. He made a sound in his throat so much like a rooster that No-Name stopped pecking and looked at him curiously. Mother laughed loudly and clapped her hands.

Finally the grain was gone, the chicken stopped

pecking, the umbrella stopped turning, the fishes stopped swimming, and Charles cranked the music box slower and slower until the song ended on a final *thunk.*

"Well, the carton of coconuts was fun, Tom, and the canoe was even better, but I think this chicken is the craziest present yet!" Mother said, delighted with her gift. She turned to Cornelia and Charles. "So what's the chicken's name?"

"It doesn't have one," said Charles. "We've been calling her No-Name, so you could name her yourself."

"What about 'Country Fried'?" said Mr. Hoover.

"What about 'Colonel Sanders'?" suggested Deeter's mom.

"Or 'Chicken Nuggets'?" said Father, laughing.

"Nobody's going to eat this chicken," said Mother. "She needs a name all her own."

"Debacle," said Cornelia.

"What?" said Mother.

"Debacle. After all that's happened," Cornelia said, laughing.

"The Great Chicken, Debacle," said Deeter.

"Perfect," said Mother. "Debacle it is." She turned to her neighbors. "Cornelia made me a birthday cake, and you are all invited over for cake and ice cream around seven. We won't even think about cleaning up our yards till tomorrow."

"Oh, no," said Cornelia. "Not tomorrow."

"Not a chance," said Charles.

"Never, never, never!" said Mindy.

"Why not?" asked their father.

Cornelia leaned over and thrust her face in his. "Because *tomorrow* you are taking us to Starlight Park," she said.

"To ride the merry-go-round!" cried Mindy.

"And the Red Devil," said Charles.

"And the Mad Hornet!" said Deeter.

"As many rides as we want!" Cornelia finished, already feeling her hands on the metal bar, her lips stretched thin over her teeth, and her hair blowing in the wind.

"Aha!" cried Mother. "So *that* was the bargain!"

This time Father didn't groan. He didn't moan.

"I guess I can clean up the yard any time," he said. "You've got it. Starlight Park, it is."

Cut-cut-cut-cudacket! said Debacle. And laid another egg.